The Sleuth's Dilemma

The Sleuth's Dilemma

The Librarian Sleuth—Book Two

By
Kimberly Rose Johnson

Dedication

For Trevor. You inspire me to be the best I can be.

Acknowledgments

Special thanks go to everyone who has supported and encouraged me in my writing adventures. I could not do this without you. Mari, thanks for having coffee with me and allowing me to pick your brain about the teachers and guidance counselors. You were a great help. To my critique group, your attention to detail is so appreciated. To my editor, thanks for helping to make the books the best they can be. To my Facebook readers group, thanks for being around when I'm stuck and need inspiration. To my family, thanks for always believing in me. And finally, thank you for reading. If not for you, I couldn't write because my publisher wouldn't publish my stories if no one wanted to read them.

Chapter One

Anna Plum tried not to fidget in her seat. She hated meetings after a long day of teaching, and this one in particular made her uneasy. She glanced at her co-workers, Luke Harms and Stan Gibson, who were seated around the conference room table. Why had Titus Gains, Tipton High School's newest guidance counselor, asked the English teachers to meet with him? In all the years she'd been teaching, a request like this had never come from a guidance counselor.

"Anna, Ms. Porter would like for you and Luke to co-chair this year's writing contest. Luke, you'll teach Anna the ropes?" Titus looked expectantly toward the department head.

Anna sat up from her slouched position and shot a look toward Luke. He was good at his job, but she dreaded working so closely with the man. "This is the first that I've heard I was stepping into this position. I'm not sure—"

Titus lifted a hand. "Sorry. From what I've been told the decision's been made. I'm only the messenger."

Anna's heart sank. Luke was about as much fun to work with as the Grinch at Christmas. He had no sense of humor and took life way too seriously.

Luke cleared his throat. "I've chaired the contest for the past five years and was promised by Ms. Porter I wouldn't have to do it anymore."

Anna had heard the principal say as much, but for some reason hadn't given it a second thought. Too bad this hadn't come up sooner. Maybe then they could have avoided this awkward meeting.

Titus frowned and looked at his computer screen. "Right. I remember reading that in my notes from our faithful leader. She was hoping you would do it one last year, so you could train someone else to take over."

"I appreciate her position," Luke said. "But I really can't be bothered with it this year. When I took on the advanced placement classes as well as college writing it was agreed that I would no longer chair the contest. It's a huge time drain. My classes would suffer, plus I'm in the middle of grading term papers. I understand Miss Plum will need guidance, but I wouldn't be able to give the contest, or Miss Plum, adequate attention."

Anna bit her tongue. As if she needed her hand held. She pulled her shoulders back and raised her chin.

Titus sighed.

Anna felt for him. It wasn't fair of their boss to thrust Titus into this position. He was, after all, a school counselor, not an admin, but Ms. Porter, the principal, did things her own way. Since this was the only high school in town, Anna had learned to grin and bear it, whether she agreed with a decision or not.

"Right. I forgot the reason behind you not chairing it this year. Give me a minute to re-read my notes." A couple of minutes later he looked up. "You're off the hook this year, Luke. Anna, that leaves you and Stan."

"Works for me." She grinned at Titus and did her best to ignore Luke. Though the child in her wanted to stick out her tongue at him. She giggled at the thought and slapped her hand to her mouth. Titus shot her a questioning look. "Sorry," she mouthed.

Titus sent Anna a smile that would make a movie star jealous. His flawless teeth, strong, clean-shaven jawline, and thick dark hair were perfect enough to grace the cover of any magazine. She pulled her attention away from the counselor and onto her least favorite teacher.

"Luke, I assume you don't mind being consulted if either of the newbies has a question?" A line etched between Titus's brows.

"I'll do my best." Luke shuffled through a file on the table in front of him.

"I'm sure Stan and I will be able to handle it without bothering you too much."

"Excellent." Titus shot her a half-smile. "That's all we had on the agenda today. Thanks, everyone."

Stan stood. "Anna, let's meet tomorrow after school to discuss our game plan. I need to take off right now."

"That's fine." It would give her time to dig up the rules from last year. The contest seemed to run itself when Luke was in charge. As much as she didn't care for the man, she would give credit where it was due. "Luke, before you leave, can I get the contact information for the judges?"

He shook his head. "I'm afraid not."

"Why?"

"I was the sole judge."

"You're kidding." How did he have the time? "No

wonder you don't want to keep chairing the contest. Is there a reason you did it yourself, or can I try and find judges?"

"I did it on my own because I couldn't find anyone to help." He raised a brow. "Including you, Miss Plum." He turned and left the room.

Anna's jaw dropped before she quickly shut it.

A low slow whistle grabbed her attention.

She faced Titus and scowled.

"Sorry. The tension between you and Luke is palpable. Is there something I can do to help?"

She shook her head. "No. But thanks." Luke Harms used to be a great guy before his wife drowned; but ever since, he'd become difficult. She felt sorry for him, but at the same time he annoyed her more than anyone she'd ever met.

"I see. I hope the two of you can come to some sort of truce. I'd hate to see the English department fragmented."

She gathered her stuff. "Don't worry, I know how to remain professional."

"I'm glad. Thanks for being so nice about this even though I know you don't appreciate the extra work load. Believe me, I understand getting stuff dumped on you."

Her frustration fizzled. "Now it's my turn to apologize. I didn't mean to make your job more difficult than it already is."

"No worries. This year hasn't been easy, but I like a challenge. Did you know I used to teach English Lit? If you decide to delegate and need judges, let me know. I'll take a stab at a few entries."

"Really?" Surprise filled her voice. "That's so nice.

Thanks."

"Sure. It could be fun." His deep, sky blue eyes twinkled.

Wow. How had she never noticed this man's beautiful eyes? "I...uh...should get out of here. My dog Freddy needs a walk and time to run."

He waved her ahead of him as they left the conference room. "What kind of dog is Freddy?"

"American Eskimo Spitz. He's a ball of white fur and loves nothing better than to run and play in the park." Her insides warmed thinking about her precious dog. She didn't know what she'd do without him. Freddy kept her warm at night and made her laugh when she was awake—at least when he wasn't into mischief, but even then he was often hilarious.

"I've seen those. They're cute. I have a chocolate lab. Maybe we'll see you at the park one of these days."

"Not likely with the hours you keep."

He sobered and glanced her way. "I need to work on my priorities. My first year here has been a challenge, but I feel like I know most everyone at the school now. Getting to know all the students' names has been difficult on top of a new position, but I'm getting the hang of how things are done." He continued walking toward his office, which was in the same direction Anna was heading.

"I'm glad. The students seem to really like you. But what's not to like?" She grimaced. "Sorry, I probably shouldn't have said that last part." She couldn't even look him in the eyes.

He chuckled. "I'll take the compliment."

Relief washed over her, and she grinned. "I'll see

you tomorrow."

"Miss Plum?" Lauren one of her former students waved and walked toward her.

"Hi, there." The normally happy-go-lucky girl appeared troubled.

"I've been better. Can we talk?"

"Sure." She motioned toward her classroom. Lauren had a habit of stopping in at least once a week to visit but something was definitely off today.

Titus parked his pickup along the street near Tipton Park. Rudy, his two-year-old Labrador Retriever barked.

"Hold on." He got out and patted his leg. "Come on, boy."

Rudy leapt from the cab of his pickup and danced in a circle.

Titus laughed. He closed and locked the door then jogged toward a grassy knoll. Rudy loped ahead of him a few feet. Anna's mention of her dog needing exercise reminded him it had been a while since he'd brought Rudy to a park. He tossed the ball he'd brought, and Rudy tore after it.

Titus looked around, taking in the green space. Cherry blossom buds colored the trees. Young mothers watched their little ones climb on the play equipment that would rival the playgrounds in a city twice the size of Tipton. Rudy bounded toward him and dropped the ball at his feet. "Good boy." He grabbed the ball and tossed it again.

"Well, this is a surprise."

He turned and saw Anna strolling toward him with a white ball of fluff on a leash. "I'll say. This must be Freddy."

Anna grinned, and her eyes widened. "You remember names better than you let on."

Rudy slid to a stop and dropped the ball. Then he noticed Freddy and moved close for a sniff-and-greet.

Anna watched the dogs closely. "They seem to like each other." She reached down and unhooked Freddy's leash. "Hopefully this little guy won't run off. I can't tell you how many times I've had to chase after him." She tossed Freddy's ball. "Here's to hoping."

Titus threw Rudy's ball too, and both dogs tore after the toys. "Have you made any progress on the writing contest?" He glanced her way, but kept his attention focused on the dogs.

"Not much. I printed off last year's rules. Fortunately, the deadline and rules were already posted on the school's website. So now it's only a matter of judging."

"I'm really sorry about how all of this was dumped on you. Apparently, Ms. Porter had forgotten that she'd promised Luke he didn't have to do it this year. She'd hoped he would help train you, but we know how that turned out. I suggested skipping it, but apparently this contest is a huge deal to a lot of the students."

"It is, and I wouldn't want to see it go away, but I sure wish I hadn't had that contest dropped on me at the last minute. I feel so behind already. There's a lot that I should've been doing in preparation, but now I have to wing it. Not my favorite way of doing things."

Anna looked wistfully toward the dogs as they trotted back to them.

"I would imagine not. If there was any other option..."

Anna shook her head. "Sorry, I know it's not your fault. I won't complain again. I promise." She crossed her heart with her pointer finger.

He chuckled. "Relax, Anna. I don't mind a little venting. I wasn't all that happy when I was told I had to run the meeting. It doesn't fall under my job description."

"I'm afraid Ms. Porter is like that. You'll get used to the way she does things."

The dogs lost interest in chasing their balls and began to follow their noses around the park. "Think we should trail them?"

"Probably." She sauntered after the animals.

He kept pace. "Tell me about Tipton."

She shot him a startled look. "You've lived here since August, haven't you? That was seven months ago."

He nodded. "I don't get out much."

"What do you want to know?"

He shrugged. "Anything. I've been married to my work, and other than trips to the grocery store and coffee shop, I haven't been out. What do people do here for fun? Where are the best places to eat?"

"Hmm. Well, it depends on the time of year. At Christmastime, there's the annual tree lighting and Christmas caroling around the tree along with hot chocolate and cookies. But the spring is iffy, as I'm sure you've noticed. The cherry blossom festival was cancelled due to lack of funding. In the summer months, there's a movie in the park on Friday nights. That's always a hit. And in the fall, there's a harvest festival. You didn't go to that?" She glanced his way.

"I'm afraid not. Like I said, I've been immersed in work. But I've noticed the people here are friendly—at least they are now." He chuckled. "When I first arrived, it was awkward."

"What do you mean?" Anna whistled. Freddy looked up then trotted their direction.

"The day I arrived I went to Roaster's Coffee, and everyone stopped what they were doing to stare at me."

Anna's eyes widened. "What did you do?"

"I figured they were probably curious, so I introduced myself as the guidance counselor at the high school."

"That was smart." Admiration filled her voice. "Then what happened?"

"Everyone went back to their business, and the owner of the place gave me a coffee and donut on the house as a welcome to town."

"That sounds like Pepper."

He wouldn't know, and to his shame, he had assumed she was hitting on him. Guess not. His face heated. He cleared his throat. "So how long have you been teaching at the high school?"

"This was my first job after graduating with my masters."

He'd do the math if he had a clue how old she was. "So that makes what, five years?"

She laughed. "I knew I liked you. Sure, let's say five." Freddy leaned against her leg and looked up at her. "Looks like he's ready to head home."

"Yeah, I suppose Rudy is too." They walked toward the sidewalk. "Guess, I'll see you at work."

She nodded. "You asked about places to eat. Pretty much anyplace in town is good, but Daisy's Diner is a favorite of mine because they use fresh ingredients. Daisy grows them year round in her greenhouse and garden."

"Thanks for the tip." He unlocked his pickup and noted Anna kept walking. "Did you drive here?"

She turned back to face him. "We walked. Normally my neighbor and I walk together, but she couldn't today."

"Would you like a ride?"

"Thanks, but it's so nice, I'd rather walk."

He nodded. Anna was an interesting lady. He'd like to get to know her better, but he had to walk a fine line. He enjoyed his job and didn't want to do anything to jeopardize it. Besides, he'd heard through the grapevine that Anna didn't date—another thing they had in common. He knew why he didn't date, but why didn't Anna?

Chapter Two

Nancy Daley locked up the library and set out on foot for home. Spring in Oregon wasn't always this sunny, and she intended to enjoy every minute even if there was something weird going on at the library. A dog barked, drawing her attention. "Well, if it isn't Freddy." She waved toward her friend and neighbor, Anna. "Are you headed home?"

"We are. Looks like we'll get that walk in after all."

Nancy came into step with the duo. "Seems so." Although it wouldn't be the power walk they normally did. "What brings you and Freddy downtown?"

"The park."

Nancy raised a brow. "That's not normal, is it?"

"Not really. It sounded like a good idea today though. As it turned out, a guy from work was there with his dog."

Something in the tone of Anna's voice put Nancy on alert. Could the confirmed bachelorette have finally met a man she was interested in—not likely, but something was different about her friend. "A teacher?"

"No. The new guidance counselor. I suppose he's not new anymore, but this is his first year. Do you know Titus Gains?"

This must be the Mr. Gains she'd overheard a couple of high school girls talking about in the magazine section. "No, but I heard he's cute."

"Cute? Hardly." Anna shook her head. "He's too...manly to be cute." A twinkle lit her eyes.

"You like him." Nancy grinned.

"I didn't say that."

"You didn't have to."

"I work with him."

"So?"

"So, it's...it's—"

"It's what?" Nancy teased.

"It's a bad idea to go there."

"I don't see why. He's a single man. You're a single woman. He's *manly*. You're a doll. What's the problem?"

Anna giggled. "Oh, stop it. I'm not a doll, and he's not interested."

"How do you know? You have beautiful green eyes and a baby face surrounded by gorgeous auburn hair. The definition of a doll to my way of thinking."

Anna's face reddened. "Thanks. That's sweet of you to say. But can we please change the subject?"

Nancy should show mercy to her friend, but this was the first eligible bachelor that Anna had ever seemed the slightest bit interested in. "I recall you once telling me you were open to the idea of marriage."

"Sure, but that doesn't mean Titus is the man."

"Fair enough, but he *is* the first man that I know of who has grabbed your attention."

Anna didn't respond, and Nancy knew she'd given her friend more than enough to think about. She stopped at the edge of Anna's driveway. "Are you free to walk tomorrow?"

"I don't know. I'm co-chairing the writing contest at the high school this year. I might have a meeting.

I'll text you." Anna headed toward her front door.

"Sounds good." Disappointment struck Nancy. Ironic too, considering she'd once resented having a walking partner. Anna had definitely grown on her. She set off for her own house and did a double take. A Dodge Dart sat parked in front of her house—Carter. Her stomach flipped, and she rushed toward the car. What was he doing here?

The driver's side door opened, and her boyfriend got out with his lips tipped into a frown. "Everything okay? I thought we had a dinner date."

Nancy blew out her breath. She'd forgotten. "Other than my mind being filled with too much, everything is fine. Would you like to come in? It'll only take a few minutes for me to change."

"Sure. But first." He pulled her toward him and placed a tender kiss on her lips. "I've missed you." His cerulean blue eyes showed sincerity.

She ran her hand through his thick dark hair. "We saw each other yesterday." She rested her hands on his shoulders. She liked that he was only four inches taller than her five-foot-eight frame. They were the perfect match as far as she was concerned.

"The sheriff's department doesn't count."

"Good point." She grasped his hand. Her sheriff deputy boyfriend and sheriff mother demanded complete professionalism when on the job. "Let's go inside. I'll hurry." Should she tell him about what happened at the library today? Things finally seemed to be back to normal in town, but now books were missing. Granted, the books in question were slated to be pulled from the shelves and sold at the book fair this spring so it wasn't a huge loss.

Nancy unlocked the door to her house and went inside. "Be right back." She rushed to her room and quickly changed into jeans and a lightweight lavender sweater, then freshened her makeup. After taking a calming breath, she went back to the living room where Carter waited. She caught her breath at the sight of him. It was difficult to believe her long lost childhood friend was back in her life. "I'm ready. Where are we going?"

"I thought we'd try that new Italian place that opened last week."

"Yum. I love Italian." She grabbed her purse and headed out.

Carter's hand rested on the small of her back. "So, what's on your mind that you'd forget our date? It's not like you." He held the car door for her.

"True. I'll tell you once we get on the road." She ducked and settled into the passenger seat.

Carter joined her, started the engine, then pulled out.

"I was stacking books today—"

"I thought that was the librarian assistant's job."

"Technically it is, but as head librarian I can stack books if I choose." She shot him a smug look. "May I continue?"

"Of course." He chuckled.

"Anyway, I noticed a couple of books were missing, and in their place were envelopes each containing a poem."

"Poems?"

"Yes, poorly written ones too."

"Do you think Maddie is up to her pranks again? With her dad being an English teacher it kind of makes sense."

"I hadn't thought of her, but considering her love of books, pranks, and copious amount of time she spends in the library, she would be a strong suspect. Thanks."

"No problem. I assume you won't be filing a police report."

"I don't think so. The books were shelf-worn and due to be replaced anyway. However, if the pranks escalate or something of value is taken, I'll let you know."

"Want me to ask Maddie about it? She and Gavin study together at least twice a week."

"No. I'll bring it up the next time I see her." Why hadn't she thought of the teen? It wasn't all that long ago the girl had dressed up the statues of the town's founders in period clothing along with a few other harmless pranks.

Carter pulled into the parking lot of Little Italy housed in a brick building on the main drag. "Lyle said he had the chicken fettuccini, and it was excellent."

"Good to know." The sheriff's department commander didn't hand out compliments lightly. If he said it was good, then she'd be sure to try the dish. Nancy thrust her door open before Carter could run around and open it. Although a nice gesture, she was perfectly capable of opening her own door.

Carter stood at the hood of his car. "I forgot to mention, I invited a friend to join us."

Carter had never invited another couple along—not that they'd been dating long, but this couldn't be a good thing if he didn't want her all to himself. "This is a double date?" Nancy's voice hitched.

"Actually, no."

Nancy stopped before entering the restaurant. "Okay. I'm confused. What's going on?"

"I invited a friend of mine to join us. He was supposed to bring a date, but sent a text a short time ago that he didn't have one."

"Then why is he coming?"

"Because I want you to meet him. You know practically everyone in town, and I thought you could introduce him to a few people. He's been here since shortly before I moved to Tipton, and he has no social life."

Confusion filled Nancy. She spent most of her days in the library, but she felt like she had a good handle on the town's citizens. "Who exactly are we meeting?"

"His name is Titus. We met at the Roaster's Coffee a few weeks ago and struck up a friendship. He spends most of his time working, and I knew you could help him. Honestly, I'm not sure if he'll even show."

"Okay. But for the record, this is weird."

"I guess, but I think you'll like him. He just needs more friends."

Nancy tried to squash her disappointment. Tonight wasn't turning out at all like she'd expected. Sure, she'd temporarily forgotten about their date, but she had been looking forward to it. She grasped Carter's hand. "Let's go meet your friend before he thinks we stood him up—assuming he's here." They walked hand-in-hand into the restaurant.

Nancy's eyes widened at the marble floors and

crystal lighting. "I think I'm underdressed." How had she not heard this place was so elegant? She wasn't aware Tipton had any upscale restaurants.

"I'd say everyone here is underdressed." He spoke softly near her ear. "Lyle didn't mention it being so fancy."

Nancy let out a slow and low whistle. "It looks more French than Italian."

A teenage hostess approached. "Table for two?"

Carter told her they were meeting someone.

"Mr. Gains?"

Carter nodded.

"Right this way."

They followed the girl past several candlelit tables. She stopped beside a table for four. "Your waiter will be by shortly."

Nancy's eyes widened. Gains? As in Titus Gains, the new guidance counselor at the high school? She should have realized that was who Carter had been talking about when he mentioned his first name. She sat to his left. No wonder Anna was interested in him, but she could also understand why she might shy away from him. He had a commanding presence about him.

"Titus, this is my girlfriend, Nancy."

"It's great to finally meet you. Carter has only brought you up about two dozen times in the past few weeks."

Nancy's pulse fluttered. "Seriously?"

Carter cleared his throat and coughed, "Rat."

Nancy chuckled. "Where're you from, Titus?"

"Portland."

"Did you experience culture shock when you

moved here?"

"A little, but I spend most of my time at the high school."

She nodded in understanding. "A good friend of mine teaches English there. I'm sure you know Anna Plum."

His face brightened. "Yes. In fact, our dogs played together in the park."

"Why didn't you invite her to join us?" Carter studied the menu.

"We work together, and I don't want things to get awkward between us."

Nancy's gaze shot to Titus's. "Why do you assume things will get awkward?"

His face pinked slightly. "I asked around a little about her, and from what I've been able to find out, she doesn't date. I figured she'd be uncomfortable around me if I asked her to dinner."

"I'm sure her not dating has more to do with not having the right man ask her. And she's too old fashioned to ask anyone out anyway." Nancy turned her attention to the menu before she said something stupid that would embarrass Anna.

Titus nodded. "I can see that about her, but I'm honestly surprised she's not attached romantically already." He shrugged and focused his attention on Carter.

Nancy liked this guy. She'd had the same thought about Anna—she should have found her Mr. Right a long time ago but being jilted at the altar is bound to have a long-lasting effect on a person—plus most of the eligible bachelors in this town knew her history and stayed away since she put them all in the friend zone. No matter, Anna deserved better anyway.

Nancy listened as the men exchanged stories about things that had happened while on the job. Maybe she shouldn't be surprised, but Titus's stories were as entertaining as Carter's. Who would have known a career as a school counselor could be so exciting?

An hour later Carter placed his napkin beside his plate. "Tonight has been fun, but I need to get Nancy home. Thanks for meeting us, Titus." He pushed his chair back and stood.

"Thanks for inviting me and for not making me feel like a third wheel."

"I'm glad you came." Nancy truly meant those words, and one way or another, she'd figure out a way to set Anna up with Titus.

Chapter Three

TWO WEEKS AFTER HAVING THE WRITING contest dropped in her lap, Anna pushed back from the computer in her classroom and sauntered through the hall.

"Hey, Miss Plum." Isaac, a senior and one of her former English students leaned against a locker talking with Tony, one of her all-time best students—a true wiz in everything academic.

"Hi, gentlemen. Why are you still here?"

"I forgot something in my locker," Tony held up a book. "Isaac's my ride and brought me back."

She nodded. "That was nice of you, Isaac. Have a good afternoon, boys." Her boots clipped along the floor as she made her way to Luke's room. It was past time to go home, but knowing the department head, he'd still be there. The light shone in his room. She pulled open the door and went inside. "I'm glad you're here. I have a problem."

Luke looked over his shoulder from where he stood at the whiteboard. "What's wrong?"

"I can't get any of the contest entries to pull up on my computer."

He frowned. "Hold on a second while I finish this."

She sat in a student desk near his. "There weren't as many submissions this year as in previous years."

"I heard. Stan said the same and mentioned you decided to run the contest by yourself."

"That's correct." It wasn't that she wanted to, but

Stan had an excuse about why he couldn't meet or do this or that every time she tried to get together and discuss the contest, and she'd had such high hopes for him. She'd finally given up and said she'd run it alone.

"You can handle it. You're well organized, and your students love you."

"Who are you and what have you done with Luke Harms?" She studied the man she'd known for years. His hair looked distinguished with a smattering of gray in spite of needing a trim. He wore a long-sleeve blue dress shirt with a boring tie and tan slacks that seemed a little baggy. Actually, now that she was paying attention, she realized the paunch that used to be in his gut was missing. When had he lost so much weight? Clearly, she paid little attention to the man.

Chuckling, he put the cap on the pen then turned to face her. "I know we butt heads a lot, but I respect your work, and I'm sorry I've given you the impression I don't. I also appreciate how you've reached out to my daughter. Maddie talks about you all the time. She loves leading the book club."

Anna warmed under his praise. "Thanks. Maddie's a nice girl. In spite of everything, you've done a good job raising her."

"I can't take credit for that. She had a wonderful mom." He sighed and sat behind his desk. "As I'm sure you noticed, I checked out after my wife drowned. It's only been over the past few months that things have felt like they're looking up."

"Why's that? What's changed?" His daughter had gone through a pretty traumatic experience this past fall, so maybe that had awakened the father inside him—about time too, as far as she was concerned.

"I realized my daughter needed me, and if I didn't get my act together I was going to lose her too." His soulful green eyes grabbed her attention.

She bit her lip. It seemed she might have misjudged the man. But time would tell.

"I owe a debt of gratitude to you. I was lost in my grief, and I know if it wasn't for people like you, I might have lost *her* too."

A stiff wind could have blown Anna over. "It was an honor to be there for Maddie, and I'm glad to see you're moving forward with your life."

He looked down as if embarrassed. "So, what's the problem with the entries?" His fingers tapped the computer keys.

"They're gone. I posted the finalists on the announcement board as well as on the English department's page on the school website yesterday. Today I went to print off the entries so I could read them to my English Lit class, and I can't find them. Not only that, I can't pull up the scores. Too make matters worse, the hard copy I had up in the hall is gone, and it's no longer on the website."

"Where did you have them stored?"

"On my computer."

"They aren't in a cloud or on the school network?"

"Honestly, I'm not a techie. I have no idea."

"Okay. Hold on a second." He continued to tap the keys on his computer and studied the screen for a minute, then pushed back from his desk. "Let's go check your computer. I'm not seeing anything in the file I used to save to the school's network."

"Is that bad?" Panic set in. What would she do? There were no paper copies since the submissions were electronic, and she hadn't wanted to waste paper printing them. She didn't even know who entered since the entries were blind and submitted by numbers not names. Plus, all the students submitted from a group email that had been set up for the purpose of the contest.

"Don't panic yet, Anna."

How could he sound so calm? She walked back to her classroom with Luke by her side. "Have you ever heard of something like this happening before?"

"I've misplaced things on my computer. Hopefully that's all the problem is." He sat at her desk and woke up the computer.

"Come to think of it, so have I." Hope filled her as she watched him click to her files.

She did not want to botch the contest. A five-thousand-dollar scholarship was riding on this for one of their students. The fund had been started ten years ago by the parents of a student killed in a car accident. They wanted the memory of their daughter and her love of writing to continue and had invested wisely to provide the scholarship each year.

Five minutes later Luke sat back and frowned. "It's time to call IT. I'm not an expert, but it's as if they were never on your computer."

"I had them all in one file. Did you check the recycle or trash bin?"

"First place I looked." He stood. "I'm really sorry I couldn't be much help." His brow scrunched.

Butterflies took residence inside. If he was worried, then she definitely had reason to be concerned. "It's okay. Thanks for trying."

"Figured I owed you at least that much, considering you had this contest dumped in your lap because of me."

"Thanks." Anna almost couldn't believe this was the same man she'd worked with for years. She'd spent so much time avoiding him, she hadn't realized how much he'd changed over the course of the school year. It was clear that the incident involving his daughter back in the fall had made a huge impact on him. She imagined having one's daughter held at gunpoint would jolt anyone. Even a man lost in grief.

She glanced at the clock on the wall above her whiteboard. "It's too late to reach IT. I'll have to deal with them tomorrow."

"In the meantime, you get the night off."

"Hardly. You know better than that. A teacher's work is never done."

His face lit. "Don't I know it? Good luck."

"Thanks again." She didn't believe in luck and put her hope in the Lord, but considering this was the nicest thing Luke had done for her in years, she would accept his gesture of kindness.

"Don't worry, Anna. These things have a way of working out one way or another."

"I hope you're right," she said to his back as he left the room. She looked around her classroom one last time before heading out. The desks were set in groups of four—something new she was trying, to help facilitate book discussions. The door and windowless walls had fun posters with clever quotes, one wall was set up with computers and the opposite wall held a built-in bookshelf filled with books.

She hated clutter, so kept projects to a minimum. Maybe she should give extra credit to the student who was able to locate the contest entries—since Tony was a wiz at everything, maybe he could help. She shook away the ridiculous thought. Giving a student access to her computer was out of the question.

"Time to call it a night." Freddy would be anxious for her attention anyway. She flipped the light switch then locked the door to her classroom.

"Anna! Hold up a minute."

She glanced over her shoulder and spotted Titus jogging her way. Worry covered his face. Her heart skipped a beat. "Everything okay?"

"I don't know. You need to see this." He pulled out his phone and in a matter of seconds had an email pulled up on the screen. "Miss Plum made a big mistake. Now she'll pay."

Anna shivered and crossed her arms. Why would anyone threaten her? Unease filled her. She looked around to see if someone was lurking nearby.

"Any idea what that's about?" His brow furrowed. "Or why it was sent to me?"

"None. But it gives me the creeps." Her body trembled as she wracked her brain for an incident with a student and couldn't come up with one. "It must be a student who knows you though."

"Perhaps, but the threat has me concerned. My buddy is a cop. I thought I'd run it by him to get his take on how we should respond."

Surprise filled her mixed with a little hope that this could be resolved quickly. "Thanks. And I'll ask my friend Nancy. Her mom is the sheriff."

"That's right. I forgot. Nancy mentioned that you

were friends."

"You know her?" This was an afternoon of surprises! The town was small, and Nancy was the head librarian at the Tipton Library, but Titus didn't get out much from what he'd said.

"Yes. She's my buddy's girlfriend."

"Oh. So you're going to talk to Carter." The tension in her shoulders eased slightly. "I didn't realize you were friends."

He nodded. "At the very least, the police should be aware of what's going on. I'll walk you to your car. I don't mean to frighten you, but this email made me uneasy, and I'd feel better if you aren't alone in the parking lot."

She'd been teaching at Tipton High for years without any trouble. Why all of a sudden was someone angry enough to threaten her, and why didn't they simply come to her with their grievance so she could address it? What had changed? "I appreciate the concern and the escort, but I wonder if this has anything to do with the writing contest."

He pushed the door open. "After you."

"Thanks." She walked beside him toward the parking lot and explained about the missing files. They stopped beside the hood of her car.

"I don't see how one could have anything to do with the other if the only people who know are Luke and now me."

"True. But what else did I mess up?"

He tucked his hands into his pockets and tilted his head. "I don't know, but if you figure it out, be sure to fill me in."

"I will. I suppose this kind of thing happens all

the time."

He shook his head. "Thankfully, no."

Unease gripped her. "Oh. So...have you ever dealt with an email threat directed at a teacher?" She held her breath.

"No. Maybe you inadvertently offended a student, and they need time to cool off."

She let out her breath in a puff. "Okay, but I can't imagine what I could have said or done." Her gazed slammed into his. "I handed back a test today. A couple of students didn't do well. Maybe that's it."

"Could be that a student overreacted to a test, and this will blow over, but to be safe pay attention to your surroundings, and if you feel uneasy or threatened call 911."

Now she was officially freaked out. Surely this kid wouldn't do anything to harm her physically.

"I'll see you tomorrow, Anna."

"Okay." She moved to the car door and took a moment to scan the parking lot. No one lurked. The sound of a ball hitting a metal bat made her jump. *Take it easy girl.* She chuckled as she opened the door and climbed in. Unease slithered over her.

Chapter Four

Titus sat in a cozy chair facing the stone-covered fireplace in Roaster's Coffee. A fire crackled, and the dull roar of voices filled the homey coffee shop. The soothing music coming from the overhead speakers ought to calm him, but ever since he'd read that email he'd been uneasy. He'd played it down with Anna, but he was worried. He'd seen evil first hand and hoped he was overreacting.

He glanced over his shoulder and spotted Carter walking in. He stood and raised a hand so his buddy would see him then sat and resumed staring into the fire.

Carter eased into the chair beside his and shifted to face him. "Your message sounded urgent. What's up?"

He pulled the email up on his phone and handed it over. "I received this in my inbox today."

Carter frowned as he gave it back. "What does Anna say?"

"She's as stumped as me. Do you think we should be concerned?" His heart thumped hard as he leaned forward.

"It's best to take all threats as serious. If you forward the email, I'll see what I can find out."

He let out an unsteady breath. "I was really hoping you'd think it wasn't anything."

"It might not be anything serious, but I like to err

on the side of caution."

"Good." If he'd done that with Lizbeth, she might still be alive.

Carter eyed him. "You seem rattled. Is there more?"

"No. This email is...stirring up something from my past."

Carter shifted. "I'm not a counselor, but I'm good at listening."

Titus shook his head. "Some things are best left in the past."

"Except, based on the look in your eyes, it's still haunting you."

Titus jerked his chin up slightly and kept his tone low. "I don't want to talk about it." Talking wouldn't bring back Lizbeth, and it sure wouldn't ease his guilt.

Carter shrugged. "Suit yourself."

"Thanks." Titus pushed the memories aside. "I reported the email to the school district earlier today, and their cyber expert is supposed to get back to me tomorrow. I didn't tell Anna I involved them though."

Carter nodded. "Keep me updated on what you learn. I don't know Anna well, but from what I've seen, she's a strong woman, I think you can be upfront with her."

"Good." He downed the last of his decaf coffee. "I never expected to be dealing with this sort of thing in Tipton."

"I hear you. When I moved here this past fall I said much the same. Goes to show that it doesn't matter the size of a town, criminals live everywhere."

"I suppose so."

"Anything else going on at the school that

concerns you?"

Titus sat upright. "No. Is there something you know that I don't?" What had he gotten himself into?

"Relax. It was only a question."

He really did need to relax. The past had him paranoid. "Oh, okay. Other than this email, things have been smooth." He hunched closer to Carter, keeping his voice low. "I received word that Ms. Porter won't be returning as the principal at Tipton High next year."

"Any idea who her replacement will be?"

He shook his head.

Carter sipped from his cup. "What about you?"

"Me?" Titus's voice hitched. "I'm a guidance counselor."

"True, but it seems to me you are qualified." His buddy shrugged. "From where I sit it almost seems like she's grooming you for the position."

Could Carter be right? "I've never considered becoming a principal, and she's said nothing to me." However, the idea was intriguing. "I forgot to mention, none of this is public yet, so..."

"Got it. I don't know anything." Carter titled his head. "Changing topics. I'm hosting a barbeque at my place on Saturday. You're invited. Feel free to bring a plus one. It'll be a small group. Mostly people from work and Nancy, of course."

"Thanks. Count me in." He could use the distraction. Anna's face danced across his mind. "I'm not sure about the plus one though. Text me the details."

"That's fine. There will be plenty of food either way."

"Great. Guess I should head home. I owe Rudy a walk." Titus stood. "I'll see you Saturday."

Anxiety gripped Titus as he headed for his pickup. Maybe he should give Anna a call and make sure she was okay. He'd swing by her place but didn't know her address. Even if he had her address, he didn't want to freak her out by showing up at her home—it would cause him alarm if he were in her position. He pulled out his cell phone, found her number in his work contacts, and pressed it.

"Hello?"

Relief filled him. "Hi, Anna, it's Titus."

"Oh, hi. Is everything okay?" She breathed hard into the phone.

"Uh, yeah. I was calling to ask you the same question. Did I catch you at a bad time?"

"I'm on a walk. What's up?"

"I guess that email has me a little worried, so I wanted to check on you."

"That's sweet. Thanks. I'm fine. I'm walking with Nancy Daley. You've met her?"

"I have. Okay, then. I won't keep you. Enjoy your walk, but please call me if you need anything."

"Is there something else going on? You're kind of freaking me out."

"I'm sorry, please don't freak out. You seemed upset after we talked earlier, and I simply wanted to see how you were doing."

"Oh. Well. Thanks for calling."

"Sure thing. I'll see you tomorrow." He pocketed his phone. Calling had been a bad idea. Anna wasn't Lizbeth. It was a completely different situation. Then why did it feel so similar, his pulse thrummed in his ears, and why did his gut tell him Anna was in danger?

Anna stared at the phone a moment before tucking it into her pocket.

Nancy glanced her way. "What's wrong?"

"That was Titus, from work."

"Titus?"

"Yes. He called to check on me."

Nancy's pace slowed. "That was sweet of him, but why did he think he needed to check on you?"

"I suspect that email I told you about has him more concerned than he's letting on."

"Interesting. I wonder why? Do you think he might have feelings for you?"

"No way. He's a concerned co-worker, nothing more." Anna turned and walked backward, checking out the area behind them. The quiet residential street looked the same as always. A man from a local yard maintenance company weeded a flowerbed across the street. A few cars were parked along the curb, and the sound of children playing nearby filled the air. She turned back around and walked facing forward.

"I suppose you could be right about Titus. When we had dinner with him the other night, he seemed like a nice guy. Tell me more about this writing contest."

"There's not much to it. Students enter every year with the hope of winning a five-thousand-dollar scholarship for college. It's not a lot, considering the cost of college, but every little bit helps.”

“Is it highly competitive?”

“I imagine so. This is my first year running it.”

“Maybe that’s something we need to talk to Luke about then.”

Ugh. “No, thank you. Although, to be fair he was really nice when I asked him for help today. I guess he’s not as horrible as I’d thought.”

Nancy grinned. “He’s stopped in at Carter’s place a couple of times with his daughter while I was visiting. Maddie and Carter’s nephew are practically inseparable.”

Anna grinned. “I’ve noticed the same at school. Who would’ve thought those two would be such good friends?”

“Apparently you, since you thrust them together when you asked them to head up the book club.” Nancy shot her a knowing smile.

“Perhaps, but I had no idea they’d click so well. I saw two teens in need of attention and friendship and thought they’d work well together.” The neat thing was they were best friends and not romantically involved, according to what she’d heard them say to other students who’d asked if they were a couple. It drove her crazy to see kids kissing in the hallways. Maddie and Gavin didn’t even hold hands to her knowledge.

A gust of wind sent Anna’s hair whipping into her face. She shivered as a chill raced through her. Their homes were only a house away and not a moment too soon. “Brr. I’m looking forward to summer.”

“Me too.” Nancy grabbed her arm, stopping her. “Sweet juniper. Look.”

"What?" She followed Nancy's gaze toward her garage door. She chilled at the violent message painted there. She closed her eyes blocking out the hateful graffiti. "What did I do to make someone so angry?"

"Good question." Nancy walked up Anna's driveway. "The better question is who did it." She stopped, resting her hands on her hips and turned one hundred and eighty degrees slowly. "I have a security camera positioned at my front door, but that won't help at your place. I wonder if any of our neighbors have one that would catch activity over here."

"I have no idea. I know you're really into having surveillance cameras and rightly so, considering what happened not all that long ago to you, but I never saw the need."

Nancy raised a brow. "How about now?"

"Now, I'm calling the police." With a shaky hand, she pressed the numbers on her phone's keypad then reported the graffiti. Freddy whimpered. She reached down and picked him up, drawing him close to her chest. "It's going to be okay, boy." Freddy licked her cheek.

"Let's wait in your car for the police. That big tree between our properties blocks the view from inside my house."

"You don't need to wait, Nancy. I'm sure you have better things to do."

"Nope." She shivered. "I'm going to wait with you, but in the car with the doors locked."

Anna's heart warmed. "You're a good friend, but let's go inside my house."

"I want one of the deputies to do a walk through first."

"Oh." Lightheadedness hit Anna, and she reached out to steady herself.

"Oh, dear. I didn't mean to frighten you. You're so pale I'm afraid you're going to faint." She wrapped an arm around Anna. "Come on. You need to sit. Let's go to my car."

"What about Freddy? Your car is a classic. He will make it smell like a dog and shed his white fur all over." Her friend's 1969 Mustang was her pride and joy and Anna wouldn't blame her if she didn't want her ball of white fluff in it.

"He'll be fine. We can crack a window if we need to." Nancy grabbed a blanket from the trunk and handed it to Anna. "For Freddy."

Relief filled Anna. "Good idea." At least Freddy's white hair wouldn't get all over the car with a blanket over the seat. She spread it out then plopped her little buddy onto the seat and scooted in.

Nancy sat behind the steering wheel. "It's much better in here out of the cold breeze."

A few minutes later a police car pulled up along the curb.

"Oh good, it's Lyle." Nancy opened her door. "Come on. You'll like the commander, so don't let his Navy SEAL-like appearance intimidate you."

"Okay." She'd seen the man around town many times but had never spoken to him. She followed Nancy over to the police car and noticed his nametag said Commander Griffin. It'd probably be best if she stuck to his title, considering she didn't know him like Nancy. She squared her shoulders and raised her chin. "Hi, Commander. I'm Anna Plum."

"This is your house?"

She nodded.

"Okay. Wait here while I look around outside and take some pictures."

Freddy squirmed in Anna's arms. She placed him on the ground. "You don't need to stick around, Nancy." Having Nancy by her side was a comfort, but she hated to impose on her friend.

"Will you stop? I told you I want to be here, and I have nothing else more important than this."

"Okay. If you're sure."

After about ten minutes, the commander approached them. "I have everything I need. You weren't the only one hit today. A house on the block over was as well. There was one across town too. I'm guessing you surprised them, and they had to make a run for it. I found a couple of half used spray cans on the side of the house. It looks like they'd planned on continuing over there. Did you see anyone?"

Anna shook her head. "No one. So this wasn't aimed at me specifically?"

"No. It appears to be random. All the messages are similar in nature. With as many houses as were vandalized though, I'm sure someone saw something. The other deputies and I will compare notes."

"Thanks, Lyle," Nancy said. "I was concerned someone might have broken in. Did you see any signs of that?"

"None. I don't think you have anything more to worry about. The other homes were only vandalized on the outside and no break-ins were reported. You can rest assured, knowing we'll be keeping our eyes open." He nodded toward Nancy then left.

Anna blew her breath out. "Knowing this was random and not related to what's going on at the school makes me feel a lot better." She pulled out her house key.

"Me too. That's why I didn't ask him to walk through your house. I'm sorry for overreacting earlier and scaring you. Too bad we didn't see anyone." Nancy looked around as if expecting to see someone lurking nearby.

If the situation weren't so horrible she'd laugh at her friend's overactive imagination. "I'm glad we got here when we did, or your house could have been next. I guess they started here. Has a gang moved into town?"

"Not that I've heard," Nancy said. "I'm guessing this is the handiwork of a teenager who has too much time on his hand."

"And a lot of anger too, based on the rotten words spray-painted on my garage door."

Nancy nodded. "Makes you wonder though."

"About what?"

"Whose houses were hit, and if it was as random as it appears."

Chapter Five

"HEY, LUKE." ANNA STEPPED INTO HIS classroom after school. She wrung her hands. She hated that things weren't going the way they should be, and she felt responsible.

He looked up from his computer. "Hi there, any luck with the contest entries?"

"I'm afraid I have two choices. Ask the students to resubmit or go off the original results and choose the winner based on those."

"Going off the original results won't work. Remember, you don't have them officially anymore. We'd have to take the word of the students and we simply can't. The only way this is going to work is to start the process over."

"I didn't think of that."

"Even if the finalist list hadn't turned up missing, the family who set up the scholarship fund gave specific instructions on how the contest was to be handled. If we don't do it per their instructions, the scholarship for that year will roll over into the following."

"Stink." She crossed her arms. "So my only option is to ask the students to resubmit and risk that they've made changes."

"Are you sure IT wasn't able to retrieve any of the files? They have to be on your computer somewhere."

She shook her head. "When I got to work this

morning, I had the black screen of death. My computer is toast."

His jaw slackened. "You're kidding. And I thought I was having bad luck."

"What are you talking about?"

"My house got hit with graffiti yesterday."

"You too?"

"Don't tell me your place was hit as well?"

She nodded. "I heard Stan's house has graffiti too."

He rubbed his chin. "With three teachers from the English department having their homes vandalized, it's obvious this wasn't a coincidence. He's the most popular with the students, so I'm surprised someone targeted his place."

"Maybe we aren't dealing with a student."

He lowered his chin and raised a brow. "You don't seriously believe that?"

She shrugged. "I don't know, but I agree it looks suspicious. I think we should let the police know in case they haven't already connected the dots."

"Good idea." He looked at his watch. "I'm about finished here, if you want to wait, we can go over there together."

"Or we could call."

"What's the fun in that?" He winked then returned his attention to his computer.

Luke Harms winked at her! Had the world been turned upside down? She headed back to her classroom, grabbed her stuff, then locked up. She turned from the door and nearly bumped into Titus. "Oops. Sorry about that."

"No problem. I wanted to give you an update on

your computer. It appears to have a worm. You should have your computer back on Monday. Will you be okay until then?" She walked beside him.

"I'll have to be. Thanks for letting me know. But what do I do about the writing contest?"

"We'll need to make an announcement that all entries must be resubmitted due to tampering with the entries."

"Okay. I'm not looking forward to re-judging all those entries."

Titus blew out a breath and rubbed his neck. "What a mess. Send the finalists to me once you get them judged."

"Really?" Her voice rose an octave and relief surged through her.

"Yes. It will be fun, and the students deserve fresh eyes."

"Thank you! That's so nice of you. Wait until I tell the students that you're the final judge."

"About that. Let's keep it between us."

"But, why?" Was he afraid whoever was targeting her would turn their attention to him if word got out his judging determined the winner? He didn't seem the kind of man to be afraid of anything, much less some punk kid.

"I'd rather remain anonymous."

"Okay. As you wish." Whatever his reason, she'd respect his desire for privacy.

He nodded. "I appreciate that. I don't want any students to harbor ill will toward me—I need them to trust and like me if I'm going to be helpful to them when they need guidance."

"I never thought about your job that way, but I

guess I see your point."

"All done." Luke strode toward them. "Are you ready to go, Anna?"

Titus raised a brow and kept his voice low. "The two of you are not only getting along, but hanging out together?"

She grinned. "Luke's not so bad after all," she whispered. "We're going to the police station to let them know that three teachers from the English department were victims of the graffiti yesterday."

"I hadn't heard. I wonder if any other teachers' homes were affected?" He rubbed his chin and his eyes narrowed. "I'll look into that. It might help the police tighten their search for the culprit."

Luke sidled up to them. "Exactly what we were thinking."

Nancy nodded in agreement. Was Titus bothered that no one had told him about the graffiti sooner, or was it something else? "We should be going."

Titus stepped aside allowing them to pass.

Luke held the door open for her as they left the building. "Any idea what you're going to do about the writing contest?"

"Yes. Since I don't actually have proof of which entries were finalists I have to start over and re-judge all the entries again."

He whistled long and slow. "That's a lot of work, but it really is your only option."

"I agree. But it should go much faster this time since I'll probably remember them once I start reading them again." She studied Luke out of the corner of her eye. He was quite a handsome man. His salt and pepper hair suited him and gave him an attractive, distinguished look. She shook her head. What was wrong with her lately? She hadn't given a man a second glance in years, and now all of a sudden two men had caught her eye.

Her confession to Nancy a few months ago tickled her memory. Maybe this was a natural progression after admitting her desire for marriage and a family. Perhaps she had finally healed from her former fiancé's jilting. Admittedly, she was hesitant to get involved, considering how things had turned out last time. The idea of getting dumped at the altar again was too much to bear. But, what were the chances of that happening twice to the same person?

"You okay?"

She glanced toward Luke. "Yes. Just lost in my thoughts."

Luke nodded and wondered where Anna's thoughts had taken her. The look on her face suggested she was troubled. "Anything you want to talk about?" Now why had he asked that? He didn't want to get involved with whatever it was. He had enough problems of his own.

Anna shot a look in his direction suggesting she wondered the same.

He ducked his chin. "Sorry. I know I've not been the friendliest person in the past, but you should know, I am making a concentrated effort to be more present and..." He wracked his brain for the word.

"Nice?" She raised a brow. A smile tipped up the

corner of her full lips.

He cleared his throat. "Uh. Yeah. Nice." He stopped. "Looks like we're here."

She looked toward the large stone-faced courthouse with a red roof and clock tower. "Right." She bit her bottom lip and glanced across the street away from the building. "I'm not sure about this."

"Why?"

"Well...what if the police already know?" She shook her head. "Never mind. I'm being silly. Let's get this over with."

They strolled along the sidewalk that ran between two large grassy areas in front of the courthouse. He pulled open the door. "After you."

She stepped inside. "Thanks."

The scent of vanilla and lavender wafted in the air as she passed, and he wondered what kind of perfume she wore. He generally hated the stuff, but this scent was so light and delicate he could breathe it all day and not mind. He wondered at Anna's hesitation to report what they'd discovered but decided against asking. It was clear he'd surprised her enough today, and he didn't want to scare her away now that he'd decided to move on with his life. He liked Anna. Her students only had high praise for her, and from what he'd seen, she deserved their accolades.

The door to the sheriff's department opened. A man sauntered out, nodded at them, and kept walking. They went inside and stepped up to the reception counter. He caught the woman's eye. "Hi. We have information regarding the graffiti found on several houses yesterday."

A few minutes later a deputy opened a door that led to the bullpen. "Anna. This is a surprise." He spared Luke a glance and a nod. "Luke."

Anna stood. "Hi, Carter. Are you handling the graffiti case? I thought Commander Griffin was."

"How's it going?" Carter shook Luke's hand, then turned his focus back to Anna. "It's actually my case. The commander stepped in yesterday to help due to the volume of calls we received—not all about the graffiti, mind you. Come on back. We'll talk in the conference room."

They followed him to a plain room that housed a single table with several chairs and a whiteboard.

Luke shouldn't have been surprised that Anna knew the deputy, but he was. He had become acquainted with Carter several months ago under rather unpleasant circumstances. He hadn't handled it very well—another regret.

"Have a seat." Carter sat across from them. "So what's going on?"

"Anna and I realized this afternoon that all the teachers in the English department had homes that were vandalized with graffiti."

Anna nodded. "And we thought it might be significant. Especially considering..."

Carter scribbled something in his little notebook.

What was Anna talking about that she wouldn't say? Whatever it was, Carter seemed to already know about it. "Considering what?"

Anna's brow furrowed. "It's nothing."

Clearly neither of them was going to share. He had only himself to blame. It would take time for people to see the new him. Who was he kidding? He might never be given a chance to show he'd changed, and he couldn't blame them. He'd been cantankerous and antisocial for years. He only hoped Anna wasn't one of those people who couldn't see the new him.

She had every right to be though—he'd been harsh with her on more than one occasion.

"Do either of you have any idea why the English department might have been targeted?"

Anna shrugged. "All I can think of is the writing contest."

"Hmm." Luke rubbed his chin. "There have been some issues with the contest this year." He faced Anna. "Do you really believe the two are related?"

"It's the only thing I can think of," Anna said softly.

Sadness filled her eyes. He wanted to reach out and grasp her hand to offer comfort and support but feared she'd reject his gesture. He had to help her somehow. "Do you think it's because I'm not in charge anymore?"

Carter's gaze landed on him. "You usually run the contest?"

He nodded.

"I didn't realize." He wrote on his notepad again. "And it's always gone off without a hitch?"

"If you don't count the fact that I was the sole judge and never had any help, then yes."

"Are the students aware that you were the only judge?"

"It wasn't a secret." What was Carter getting at?

"I wonder." Carter tapped his pen against the pad. "I'm not a writer or a creative person, but it seems to me that students talk. What if they've figured out what you like and were writing to appeal to you, and now with Anna in charge they were thrown for a loop."

Anna gasped. Her gaze slammed into his. "This is all my fault."

Chapter Six

"Hey, beautiful." Carter kissed Nancy's cheek.

Nancy looked around the library to see if anyone noticed. Thankfully no one seemed to be paying them any special attention. "What brings you here?"

"I wanted to check with you in case you'd discovered any more books missing."

She pushed back from her desk and stood. "Let's go ask Tara. I haven't, but she spends more time in the stacks than me." Her boots clicked on the floor as they passed the non-fiction stacks and then the Christian fiction. A woman with short blonde hair stood at the first stack of general fiction. It took a moment to register it was Tara. Nancy was still getting used to her assistant's new cut and color. "There she is."

Tara turned their direction. "Did you need me?"

Nancy motioned for her to come closer. "Have you discovered any more books missing with poems left in their place?"

"No. And I've been pulling the old books you've asked me to set aside for the book sale next month. If any more turn up, I'll be sure to let you know."

"Okay. Thanks." Nancy should be relieved, but she was a little disappointed. A good mystery was always fun and helped the time go faster on slow days at the library. "I'm going to take a break. Will you come up to the front while I'm away?"

"Sure."

Nancy slid her hand into Carter's. "Let's go for a stroll."

He raised a brow but remained silent. They went outside into the cool spring air. "Do you want to sit in the sunshine or walk?"

"I've been sitting too much today." She guided him to the right of the library away from downtown. "I talked with Anna last night. She's really concerned."

"She has reason to be." Carter looked over his shoulder and took in the area around them, then lowered his voice. "Between you and me, I think she's being targeted by an angry student."

"But why?" Nancy wanted to believe her friend was overreacting, but Carter never overreacted when it came to the job. Now to figure out a way to help Anna.

"From what I've been able to gather, the writing contest at the school is high stakes since there's a five-thousand-dollar college scholarship attached to it. I'm running with the idea that whomever is threatening her—"

"Wait. Someone has threatened her?"

"Yes. I assumed you knew."

She frowned. Poor Anna. She loved her job and her students. A threat would not only scare her but hurt her feelings. "I'd like in on this one."

"What?" Alarm filled his voice.

"I want to consult on Anna's case."

He shook his head. "Absolutely not. It's too dangerous."

"All the more reason to let me help. Anna is my friend. We both know you're stretched thin with your caseload." She softened her voice. "Let me help. Please." She batted her lashes.

He chuckled. "Not fair." He dropped a kiss on her forehead. "I'll think about it."

"Thanks." She knew he'd say yes. He couldn't say no to her—at least she hoped he couldn't.

"I'll have to run it by the sheriff too."

"Oh." Her shoulders slumped slightly. After Nancy had missed being struck by a bullet a few months ago, her mom had been overly protective and hadn't given her any consulting work with the department. No doubt that was why she was hoping the poem-writing book thief hadn't been a one-time deal.

He chuckled. "Aw, come on. Don't be like that, Nancy. I shouldn't have brought up Anna's case. I'm sorry."

Her heart melted at his contrition. "I know you're looking out for me, and I want you to feel free to discuss anything with me if it'll help you, but it's torture to have this dangled in front of me and not be allowed to get involved."

He sighed. "We want you to be safe."

"I'm a grown woman. I can take care of myself."

"Right. Like you did—"

"Don't." She winced. If one more person reminded her about that night she'd scream. It's not like she was held at gunpoint on a regular basis. It was a fluke. She'd been consulting with the Tipton Sheriff's Department for years without incident. "That was a unique situation, and you know it. This is completely different."

"I don't want to argue with you. Let's agree to disagree on this. I promise I'll consider your request to consult, and I'll let you know."

She blew her breath out in a huff. "Fine." She turned and headed back in the direction they'd come. "My break's about over."

He sighed. "Don't be angry with me."

"I'm not. I'm frustrated." Maybe having a cop for a boyfriend was a bad idea. If they weren't dating, then he wouldn't feel the need to be so protective. She knew she could win her mom over to her side, but Carter was stubborn. She watched him from the corner of her eye. Would she really have to choose between the man she cared for deeply and her passion for solving mysteries?

Later that day, Nancy pumped her arms and walked at a fast clip beside Anna. "You've really come a long way since we first started walking together a few months ago."

"I have, haven't I? I didn't even realize how much easier it is to keep up with you. Now that you mention it though, my clothes are getting a little baggy."

"Sounds like a good excuse to go shopping." Shopping wasn't her favorite pastime, but she'd enjoy helping Anna refresh her wardrobe. "How about we plan a trip to Portland and get you a new wardrobe?"

Anna laughed. "I don't think so. I'll visit the consignment shop here in town sometime soon and see if I can find a few treasures."

"Come on. It'll be fun." Nancy glanced toward a

passing car. The person inside waved, but she had no idea who they were.

"No way. I'm not wasting my hard-earned money on a new wardrobe when I'm still losing weight. Besides, vintage is in style."

"I suppose you're right. Mind if I tag along?" It wasn't like she had anything better to do.

"Not at all. Why the sudden interest in my wardrobe?"

"Beats me. I guess I'm bored." She needed something more to occupy her mind.

"Working full time, teaching Sunday school, and your social life aren't enough for you?"

"I guess not. Who knew?" Nancy shrugged.

Anna chuckled. "Nancy, you're too much. I'd love to have your life."

"You would? Why? Not that my life is horrible or anything, but you have a great one."

"I'm grateful for my job and my friends, but I want more."

"More as in a man?"

"Yes." Anna shrugged. "I'm lonely. As much as this whole thing at the school is bugging me, it's made me realize how much I want to find love again. I want someone to share my life with."

The longing in her friend's voice melted Nancy's heart. She had no idea Anna was lonely. If only there was something she could do. "I can't help with the romance, but I'd like to help find whoever is behind the contest heist."

Anna grinned. "I suppose it was a heist. I like the way you word things, my friend. You want to help me figure out this mystery?"

"I thought you'd never ask!" If the police wouldn't let her consult in an official capacity, she'd help her friend on her own until Carter and her mom agreed to include her officially. "What clues do you have?"

Anna's pace slowed. "I'll have to think about it and make a list. My guess is he or she felt they should win the contest, otherwise why get so angry? This is personal for him, and he's making it personal with me."

Nancy shivered. No wonder Carter didn't want her involved.

Anna sat at the kitchen table in Nancy's house with a piece of paper and a pen. While Nancy was showering, Anna worked on her list of clues.

Probably enjoys writing

Temper

Vindictive

Most likely a junior or senior

Needs the scholarship or really likes winning

Feels entitled

Tech savvy

Little to no conscience

Mean spirited

Possibly a straight A student.

She tapped the pen against the table. "What else?" They didn't have a lot of actual clues. It was too bad the tech people couldn't trace who had put the worm on her computer—maybe it didn't work that way though.

Nancy breezed into the room. Her damp hair hung loose around her shoulders. "How's the list coming along?"

Anna handed it to her. "I know I'm mostly psychoanalyzing, but it does give us a group of students to look at."

Nancy read the list out loud. "Straight A student? How do you figure?"

"Many high achievers get upset if they receive anything lower than an A. I should probably run this by Titus and see what he thinks. This is more his area of expertise. In fact, he might have some ideas on who it could be since he works with the students one-on-one frequently."

"Great idea." She handed the list back. "When do you get your computer returned?"

"Monday, and I can't wait. I didn't realize how dependent I've become on technology. Granted, it's my dependence on my devices that caused this problem."

Nancy pursed her lips.

"I know one thing for sure. When I get my computer back and the entries are resubmitted, I'm printing up a hard copy of each and every one of them. Then I'll store them in a safe."

Nancy chuckled. "That might not be necessary, but I understand your passion. Do you think Titus would mind a call this evening? I'd love to get started on this."

Anna sucked in a breath. "I don't know. I'd feel uncomfortable contacting him outside of work." Then again, he'd called her, so... "Won't this keep until Monday?" She liked Titus, probably more than she should but she'd rather leave the pursuing to him if he was truly interested. Easier to avoid heartbreak that way.

"I suppose." Nancy sighed. "What are you up to this evening?"

"Thought I'd go pick up a pizza then watch a movie. You're welcome to join me."

"I'd like that, thanks."

Relief washed over Anna. She'd put on a brave front, but truth be told, she was afraid of what the kid might do next.

Chapter Seven

"Maddie, I'm home." Luke closed the front door with his foot then headed for his office, where he dumped a stack of papers he needed to grade over the weekend onto his desk.

"I'm going to Gavin's house tonight. Okay?" His daughter stood in the doorway to his office.

He started to shake his head then stopped. "You spend a lot of time over there. How about you and I do something fun tonight instead?"

Her eyes widened then narrowed.

"You can invite Gavin along if you'd like." He'd done a terrible job with Maddie since his wife's death. An incident this past fall opened his eyes to his failings, and he wanted to do better. If only Maddie would allow him back into her life. He had a lot of time to make up for.

"Maybe. What'd you have in mind?"

Panic struck him. He had made the offer on a whim. "Anything you'd like."

"There's not much to do in Tipton."

"We could all go bowling."

She pulled out her smart phone and started texting. He presumed she was asking Gavin about bowling. A few seconds later, she looked up. "He's fine with bowling." Her eyes held suspicion. "Why are you doing this?"

He motioned toward a chair. "Come in and sit."

She frowned.

More work laid ahead of him than he realized. "I suppose we should have had this conversation months ago." He turned his desk chair to face his daughter and sat. "I know I failed you as a dad. I can't promise I'll be super dad, but my desire is to do better. There's no catch to tonight—I'm merely a dad who'd like to spend time with his daughter before he misses out completely on her growing up years. I'm sorry for not being there after your mom died." He dipped his chin, keeping his focus on Maddie.

"You really want to spend time with me?"

He nodded.

"I thought..." A series of emotions danced across her face.

"What?"

"That you..." her voice caught. She cleared her throat. "That you blamed me for Mom's death and that's why you avoided me for all those years." She swiped the back of her hand across her face.

His throat thickened. Overcome with love for his daughter, he stood, walked around his desk then knelt in front of her. "Aw, Maddie. I'm so sorry you thought that. I never blamed you. Your mom was a stubborn woman. If she didn't want to wear a life vest, no amount of cajoling would have made her."

She sniffled. "Would it be okay if we stay home tonight?"

"Whatever you want." He wrapped her in his arms and hugged her like he used to when she was little and let her cry. He swallowed back his own tears. "I love you, Maddie."

Her tears subsided, and she released her hold on

him. "I love you too, Dad." She stood and headed for the door.

"Where are you going?"

"I'm starving."

He chuckled. "Me too. But I need to go grocery shopping. How about we grab a pizza instead and watch something on Netflix tonight?"

She smiled. "Sounds good. I'll let Gavin know we aren't bowling. Maybe we can do that tomorrow night?" Her face lit.

"Sure. Why not?"

She did a little dance then charged off, returning a moment later. "Let's go."

He grabbed his wallet and headed for the door feeling much lighter. This was a new beginning for them.

Ten minutes later, they stepped inside Maggie's Pizza. The hum of soft voices filled the air. He walked up to the counter with Maddie by his side. "We'd like a large pizza with the works." He paid then stood aside to wait.

The door opened, letting in a blast of cool air along with Anna. His heart skipped a beat, and his pulse accelerated. What was wrong with him? Was he having a heart attack or getting sick? He felt his face with the back of his hand.

Anna walked past him, seemingly oblivious to his presence. He heard her order a large cheese pizza to go. Didn't she live alone? He couldn't imagine her putting away that much pizza all by herself.

She turned. Her eyes widened. "Well, hello." She sat down beside him on the bench across from the ordering counter.

His heart rate quickened. "Hi."

Anna waved to his daughter. "Nancy Daley and I are having a little pizza party at my place. Would you and Maddie like to join us? We've been trying to figure out who painted the garage doors."

"Yes!" Maddie blurted.

His mouth hung open a second before he remembered to snap it shut. "Are you sure, sweetie?" He'd wanted to say yes, but after their conversation earlier he figured his daughter would want time together with only the two of them.

"Of course, Dad. Can Gavin come too?"

Ah, now it made sense. "Sure." He stood. "I need to order another pizza. If Gavin is anything like I was at his age, he can eat an entire pizza all by himself."

Anna chuckled. "I've seen the kids at school eat, and I'd say you're right." She opened her purse and pulled out her wallet. "Let me help."

"Nope. I've got this." After placing the order, he returned to his seat and rested an ankle on one knee. "Maybe between the five of us, we might be able to come up with something that will help the police. I get the impression they're busy and our case isn't a priority."

Anna's brow furrowed. "Why do you say that? Carter seemed like he was on top of it to me."

Now Anna looked worried, and he was to blame. He should have kept his pessimism to himself. "In the grand scheme of crime, it seems kind of minor. Not exactly something for the major crimes division."

She nodded. "I suppose you're right, but I don't think they have a major crime division in Tipton. We aren't exactly a high-crime town."

"True, and you're probably right. By the way, I

need your address."

"Oh." She chuckled. "I suppose that would help." She rattled off her address as he typed it into his phone.

"Anna." One of the employees placed a pizza box on the counter.

"That's me. I'll see you soon, Luke." She grabbed the box then left.

Maddie bumped his shoulder with hers. "You like her."

"What?" His head shot her direction.

"You have a thing for Miss Plum."

"No I don't." *Liar.*

"Don't worry, Dad. I like her too, but not like that." She giggled. "It's okay, really."

He dropped a kiss onto the top of his daughter's head. "Thanks, but I don't think she's interested."

"You never know. She *did* invite us over."

"Exactly. Me and two teenagers along with Nancy—not exactly a romantic dinner."

She rolled her eyes. "Oh, Dad."

Wonder filled him. If someone had told him yesterday he'd be having this conversation with his daughter, much less a pizza party at Anna's house, he'd have told them they were nuts. At least his pulse had slowed, and he didn't feel clammy anymore. Had the surprise of seeing Anna walk in caused his uncharacteristic response?

Anna sent a text to Nancy. "Change of plans. Pizza at

my place. Luke, Maddie, and Gavin are joining us. Feel free to invite Carter." She should have ordered another pizza too.

She started her car and pushed the speed limit to get home. When had she last cleaned house? She liked things to be neat and tidy, but with all that had been going on a clean house had not been her top priority. How much time did she have before everyone showed?

She pulled into her driveway and cut the engine then raced inside. After putting the oven on warm, she placed the box inside then turned to take in her home. Not too bad. She grabbed a laundry basket and quickly tossed everything that didn't belong into it then rushed it to the laundry room. She always tidied the bathroom before leaving for work in the mornings so no worries there. Maybe she had time to dust and vacuum. The doorbell rang. "Or not." She pulled the door open.

Nancy stepped in. "I thought you might need a little help getting things ready."

"You're an angel in disguise." She hugged her friend. "Will you get cups and plates out and put them on the table while I vacuum and dust real fast?"

"Of course, and I'll dust."

"Thanks."

They each got busy, and a short time later, collapsed on the couch in a fit of laughter. "I can't believe we did that so fast." Freddy jumped into Anna's lap.

"Me either. But it was an adrenaline rush and kind of fun. I'm glad your house is small, otherwise we'd never have finished quickly enough."

The sound of the doorbell drew Anna's attention. "Looks like someone's here. We finished with only a minute to spare. Thanks for helping."

"No problem. You going to get the door, or should I?" She shot Anna a teasing look.

"Oops." Anna went to the door and opened it.

"Hi, Miss Plum." Maddie stood beside Gavin with Luke behind them holding two pizza boxes.

"Hi, yourself. Come in. Is your uncle coming, Gavin?"

He nodded. "He's right behind us."

She looked past Luke and spotted Carter heading up the walkway toward the door. "Welcome, everyone. Make yourselves at home. Feel free to load up and sit anywhere."

The adults ended up at the table and the teens on the floor in front of her television.

Nancy cleared her throat. "I assume we all know why we're here."

Carter raised a brow. "I thought it was for the pizza." He reached for a slice.

Nancy playfully punched his shoulder. "Well, yes. But also, to try and figure out who is behind the graffiti and writing contest snafu."

"Ha. You call that a snafu?" Anna shook her head. "That was sabotage."

"What are you talking about?" Maddie stood and walked over to the table.

Anna's gaze shot to Luke's. Didn't he tell her what was going on? "I'm sorry, I thought you knew."

Luke winced. "Miss Plum's computer was infected with a worm, and she lost everything, including all the entries for the writing contest at school."

"Oh, no! That's horrible. What're you going to do?"

Gavin sidled up to the table. "Did you know about this, Uncle Carter?"

He nodded. "But as you know, I'm not in the habit of discussing police matters with you."

"This is a police matter?" Maddie squealed. "Why are the police involved?"

Carter looked at Anna, clearly wanting her permission to share. She shook her head. If Luke hadn't told her about someone sabotaging her computer, then threatening her, he must have a good reason. "You know about the graffiti?"

The teens nodded.

"Well, all of the English teachers' homes were hit. We think it's connected to the school in some way."

"Oh," the teens said in unison.

"Have you heard any rumors at school about it?" Nancy asked as she reached for a napkin.

They both shook their heads.

Maddie snagged a second piece of pizza. "I'll see if I can find out, though."

"No." Luke's firm voice startled Anna. "I don't want you mixed up with anything dangerous."

"It's graffiti, Dad." She rolled her eyes.

"I don't care. Whoever is behind this is up to no good, and I don't want you getting anywhere near it."

"Fine." She whirled around and marched back to the television.

A weight settled on Anna. She'd thought Luke had changed, but clearly he hadn't. Then again, he was trying to protect his daughter, so maybe she should show some grace.

Luke's gaze slammed into hers. "What?"

"I didn't say anything." She kept her voice low and calm, even though her heart raced. The challenging look in his eyes made her want to lock herself in her bedroom until her guests left—she hated confrontation and avoided it whenever possible.

"But you were thinking something. I can see by the look of disapproval on your face you don't agree with me."

"I'm sorry. I suppose I'm being selfish. She's your daughter, and you know best."

He sighed then glanced toward the teens in the other room. "Do *you* think it's safe to have her go poking around in this?"

Anna shrugged. "Honestly, I don't know anymore." She looked at Carter. "What do you think? Are the kids in danger if they start asking questions around school?"

"I don't want Gavin involved, either. You made the right call, Luke."

Nancy tapped a finger on the table. "They're practically adults. I'm sure they're smart enough to keep out of danger." With a sigh she stood. "Thanks for the pizza, Anna. We can talk later." She dropped a peck on Carter's cheek then left. "I'm going home to think."

Carter's gaze followed her. "Maybe I should go help her think." He stood. "Gavin, I'll be next door when you're ready to go."

Anna's face heated as she watched Carter walk out. "I'm sorry, Luke. It seems I'm a terrible hostess."

He reached out his hand and rested it on hers for a moment. Warmth enveloped her hand. Too soon he snatched it back, probably realizing his impulsive gesture of comfort. "Their departure had nothing to do with your hosting abilities."

She nodded, instantly missing the comfort of his touch. "I imagine she's frustrated, like me. Nancy hates being told to keep her nose out of things." Was there more going on than she knew?

He chuckled. "Somehow I knew that about her. She has the curiosity of a cat, and the tenacity of a mama bear."

Anna laughed. "That describes her perfectly." She motioned toward the teens. "What are you going to do about your daughter? She's a lot like Nancy when it comes to curiosity."

"I've noticed. I wonder where she gets it? Her mom wasn't that way, and neither am I."

"Her love of reading has probably fostered her curiosity. She chooses mystery books every other month for the book club."

Surprise filled his eyes. "I should have known that."

Anna didn't reply. The man didn't need to feel worse, and she had to stop judging him. She was far from perfect and shouldn't expect him to be either, especially since he'd checked out of parenting for several years and had a lot of catching up to do. "What do we do now?"

"Now we enjoy this great pizza and watch whatever the kids have on." He slid another piece onto his plate then stood and walked into the other room.

Anna followed and sank into the couch beside him, but not too close. Talk about a turn of events. Freddy hopped up into her lap and promptly fell asleep.

"Your dog is cute," Luke said softly.

"Thanks. We're good buddies." She focused on Wheel of Fortune for the next twenty minutes and joined in with her guests in trying to solve the puzzle before the contestants.

When the show ended Luke stood. "We need to get home, Maddie."

"Okay." She stood and shot Anna a look she couldn't decipher.

What was up with that? Inviting Luke and his daughter over tonight had not been one of her better ideas. Hopefully things wouldn't be awkward at school, but she had a bad feeling.

Chapter Eight

NANCY CROSSED HER ARMS, WAITING FOR Carter to speak first as she stood at her front door. She didn't need a man to help her think, even if said man was her boyfriend. Okay, so he had saved her life once, but this was different. No one was after her. This was about the English department at the high school—at least from what she could tell.

"Mind if I come in?" Carter asked.

She stepped aside and followed him to the living room where he made himself comfortable on her sofa. She sat in the chair.

His face fell, and he rubbed the back of his neck. "I'm sorry. I didn't mean to suggest you can't think on your own. It's my nature to want to help those I care about. I suppose it's one of the reasons I went into law enforcement."

Her ire crumbled, and she moved to sit beside him. "I'm sorry for being so defensive."

"I get that. I even understand, but...it's tough having the knowledge I have. I can't help but be concerned about your safety. I'd rather you stayed out of this and leave the thinking to police. I want you to be safe."

"Wait...there's stuff I don't know? Please tell me." What wasn't he saying? "Is there more to this case than what you've told me?"

He sighed and nodded. "I shouldn't tell you this,

but a threat was made against Anna. An email was sent to Titus that stated something to the effect that she messed up and now she will pay. She has angered someone, and they are attacking."

She waved a hand. "Oh. She told me. I don't think her life is in danger, though. Do you?"

"It's hard to know anything for certain at this point. We have no suspects, and very little to go on. We need this person to make the next move. All I can say with confidence is that the circumstances surrounding the situation seem to point to an unidentified suspect who is a teen at the school, who, based on what has happened so far, appears to be angry and vindictive."

Nancy snuggled against his side and wrapped an arm across his midsection. "I already promised Anna I'd help figure out who is behind the threat. I promise to be very careful. Can we agree to disagree on my involvement in this?"

He slipped his arm around her. "I don't want to, but I can see that as long as you're breathing you're going to put your nose where it doesn't belong."

"Ouch. My nose, or rather *I*, was invited."

He chuckled and planted a kiss on said nose. "Good point."

A knock sounded on the door.

Carter let out a breath. "That'll be Gavin. Are we good?" He stood and offered her a hand up.

She took it and allowed him to pull her to standing. "Yes."

The doorbell peeled.

He glanced toward the door with annoyance. "I wish I could have you to myself a little longer."

Her insides warmed. "Me too. You'd better go though."

He nodded and walked to the door then swung it open. "You ready to go?"

His nephew nodded and walked toward Carter's car.

Carter turned to face her and drew her toward him. "Goodnight," he said softly. His soft lips caressed hers far too briefly.

"Mmm." Her eyes closed for a moment then fluttered open. "'Night." She watched him drive off before walking over to Anna's. Her neighbor's door swung wide before she even knocked.

"I was hoping you'd come back over. Is everything okay with you and Carter?" She stepped aside and motioned Nancy in.

"Yes. I'm sorry for leaving early."

Anna grinned. "But all is forgiven."

"Thanks. Do you need help cleaning up?"

"No. Carter said he was going to help you think. How did that go?"

Nancy laughed. "That's too funny. He quickly got over that idea."

"Oh. Then did Carter agree to support your sleuthing?"

Nancy grinned. "In his own way, I suppose. I know it makes him feel uncomfortable, but he respects my opinion. Plus, I understand where he's coming from. I don't like that he puts himself in danger every time he wears his uniform, so..." She shrugged.

"Good. I'm glad to have you back on my team. I'm sorry tonight didn't go like I'd hoped. Are you still up to going over that list I wrote earlier?"

"Does a mouse like cheese?"

"Eww." Anna wrinkled her nose. "What book are you reading now?"

Nancy laughed. "That's not from a book, it's from a bad poem. Now let's see that list again." She followed Anna to the kitchen.

Anna pulled it from a top drawer then handed it over. "I know our suspect list is huge. If I could give you the names of the entrants I would, but it was a blind entry. The students are assigned numbers to keep bias out of the judging process."

"I know." Nancy nibbled on her bottom lip. "I think you should check the grades of everyone who qualified to enter the writing contest and make a list of the A students. Then dig a little deeper and see if they have any disciplinary problems. I doubt this is their first act of defiance."

"Act of defiance? I'd say threatening me, hacking and sabotaging my computer, and vandalizing my house is a lot more than defiance."

"Of course. That was a poor choice of words." Nancy read through the list again. She cleared her throat. "I was a little surprised you invited Luke and Maddie over tonight."

"I know." She shrugged. "I surprised myself."

Nancy pressed her lips. She'd thought for sure her friend was interested in Titus, but if that were the case why would she entertain Luke? Then again, it wasn't a romantic evening by any stretch of the imagination. She shrugged off the thought. She held the sheet of paper out to Anna. "Maybe Titus could help you with this. You could show him your list and see if anyone comes to mind."

"Good idea. I'll do that first thing Monday."

"Great. Did you still want to watch a movie tonight?" Nancy half-hoped her friend would say no, so she could do a little research.

"Sure. Unless you're tired."

She could research later. In her life, movie nights were rarer than mysteries. "Nope. What did you have in mind?"

"North by Northwest." Anna pulled out a DVD and with the press of a few buttons, the Alfred Hitchcock movie played on Anna's flat screen TV.

Nancy's mind wandered to the case. Was the suspect male or female, what year was he, and why had he turned on Anna? Was there a connection to Luke? Hmm. That was something no one had mentioned. Everyone knew Luke ran the contest, so by him not being in charge this year things were sure to be a little different. After all, writing was subjective. She made a mental note to ask Luke if any students had brought up the contest.

As soon as the credits rolled, Nancy stood. "I should get home. Thanks for everything. Tonight was fun. Well, mostly."

Anna chuckled as she stood and walked toward the door. "Mostly the part where it was just you and me. I think I made a mistake inviting Luke and Maddie."

"And my mistake was including Carter. We should've kept it to a girls' night."

Anna's hand rested on the doorknob. "Agreed. I didn't expect Luke to react so strongly to his daughter helping. All things considered, he's never indicated he would be an overprotective parent. However, I'm actually impressed that he stood up for her. It's such a shift from the way he was at the beginning of the school year when he seemed to barely realize he had a daughter."

"What made you invite him? Just curious."

"I don't know." She tilted her head to the side. "Since the graffiti happened, we've gotten along better. He's let me see his soft side. Maybe it was a temporary lapse in judgment though, because his prickly side came out tonight."

"We all have different aspects to our personality. And even though I wasn't happy with the guys, it's kind of sweet that they're so protective."

"Spoken like a woman in love." Anna grinned as she pulled open the door. "Good night."

"See you." Nancy headed back to her house but couldn't get Anna's parting words from her mind. Was she truly a woman in love? She didn't even know what love felt like. How could she be sure Carter was *the one*?

Tuesday morning Nancy walked through the halls at Tipton High School alongside Titus. He'd agreed that she should visit the English classes today under the guise that she was promoting the public library. She only had to give a short pitch about the summer reading program, and then she could sit in on as much or as little of the class as she wanted. She still couldn't believe he'd been so accommodating. Even the teachers were nice about her taking up class time.

The plan had been simply to observe Anna's classes, but Titus had pointed out that the troublemaker was more than likely not one of her students since she taught Sophomore English, and only upperclassmen could enter the writing contest. After talking it over, they decided she needed to visit all the English classes this week. Thankfully, the library opened a couple of hours after school started, so Tara would only be alone until noon when Nancy would head to work.

Nancy walked into Luke Harms's class and spotted him sitting at his desk the same time he noticed her and motioned her over. "Hi, Luke. My spiel won't take more than five minutes. Thanks for agreeing to this."

"No problem." The frown on his brow said otherwise.

"Is everything okay?"

"I'm not sure. It appears that someone messed with the stuff on my desk."

"How would you know?"

"My desk is organized chaos. I know exactly where everything is in spite of how it might look to the casual observer, and things have been moved. But I don't see how. I always lock my door when I'm not here."

"I've noticed many teachers step out of their rooms from time to time during class time. Do you?"

"I suppose."

"Is something missing?"

"Not that I can tell." He glanced up at the clock. "I'll introduce you then let you start off the class.

Sound good?"

She nodded.

For the next few minutes, students shuffled in and found a seat. The bell rang for class to begin, and Luke rose. "Good morning, we have a guest today. Miss Daley is the head librarian at Tipton Public Library. I expect you to be courteous and listen to what she has to say." He nodded to Nancy.

"Hi, everyone. I'm excited to be here with you. I see a few familiar faces." She smiled. Blank stares looked back at her—tough crowd. "I'm here to tell you a bit about the library and how you can benefit. Although we have many activities throughout the year, I think you'll be most interested in our summer reading program that begins in June. I realize that's three months away, but it's never too early to be thinking about what books you'd like to read. If you can't find it at our library, I can order it for you from another one."

A female student raised her hand. "What's in it for us?"

Nancy grinned at the long-haired brunette. "I'm glad you asked. What's your name?"

"Lauren."

"Well, Lauren. There are prizes. Every time you read one hundred pages you get to enter a drawing for a prize. There are multiple prizes available that have been donated by local businesses. In past years we've had things like free ice cream cones, pizza, bowling packages, and gift cards. I'm still working on the prizes for this year." She gave the website address. "Be sure to check the calendar for upcoming events. If you happen to come into the library, please say hi and tell me that you saw me in your class. Thanks." She looked to Luke then moved to an empty desk near the door.

A few minutes before the bell rang, Nancy slipped from the class and went to Anna's room. Nancy repeated the process all morning then walked to Titus's office shortly before noon. She stood in the doorway and knocked on the frame. "Hi. Do you have a few minutes?"

Titus motioned her in. "Sure. Have a seat. How'd it go?"

"Great. Some of the students looked bored, but others appeared interested."

"Anyone grab your attention?"

"Not really. I need to process things in my mind. I'll let you know though."

"Okay."

"Have any more threats been left for Anna?"

"No." Relief shone on his face. "I can't tell you how troublesome this entire thing is. It makes me wish we could cancel the contest altogether."

"I understand. Whoever is behind the problems will get caught one way or another." Nancy had faith in the police, but she hoped to help them solve this on the sooner side. "Oh, and you might want to check in with Luke. He thinks someone was rifling through the stuff on his desk."

His brow rose. "Okay. Thanks."

Nancy stood and left. She needed to get a bite to eat and then get to work to relieve Tara. She headed to Roaster's Coffee.

Pepper White, the owner and her longtime friend, waved as she entered. "This is a surprise. It's not even Friday. What gives?"

Nancy laughed. "I thought I'd change things up this week."

Pepper's face fell. "I wish I could stop to have a coffee and donut with you right now. But the lunch rush will be in soon."

"Don't worry. I'll be back on Friday for our usual. Today I need a large coffee to go and a bagel with cream cheese."

"You got it." She filled a large paper cup with steaming coffee. "What's going on?"

"Not much." Other than her friend had been threatened, the school's computers hacked, homes vandalized, and the authorities had no idea who it could be other than most likely a student at the high school. She smiled sweetly. "I was visiting the English classes at the high school this morning to talk about the library."

"That's cool." She pressed a lid onto the cup and placed it on the counter then bagged the bagel and cream cheese. "Is that something you always do? I don't remember you mentioning it in the past."

"No. It's something new I'm trying."

"Well, I hope it increases traffic at the library."

"Thanks. Me too." She grabbed her purchase. "See you Friday." As she stepped outside, she spotted one of the kids from a class she'd been in earlier. "Hi. It's Lauren, right?"

The girl stopped before entering the coffee shop. "Yes. I have lunch release."

Nancy nodded. "Enjoy." She held up her cup and bag. "I'm eating on the run. Maybe I'll see you at the library soon."

"It's possible. A few of my friends are thinking about doing the summer reading program." She turned and walked into the coffee shop.

Nancy grinned. Today might not have pointed out the troublemaker, but it looked like it was successful in promoting the library. Her phone buzzed, announcing a text message. She pulled it out before getting back into her car and stared at the screen. Titus didn't usually text her. Odd.

We need to talk. I received a very unsettling email this morning from Anna. Titus

Chapter Nine

Titus re-read the email that Anna had printed off for the second time. "Mr. Harms should be running the writing contest. Put him in charge—or else." He glanced toward Anna who twisted her hair around her finger. Who was this kid, and why the obsession with Luke? Could Luke be in danger?

"What do you think?" Anna tapped her foot on the floor, causing the floor to shake slightly.

"I think you need to relax and not stress over this."

"Not stress?" Her voice rose. She closed her eyes. "Sorry. I didn't mean to shout. Would this kind of note upset you?"

"I'll admit it would distress me, but only because I'd be insulted." Whoever was behind it appeared to lack confidence in Anna. Why? She was well liked—at least he thought she was. "Have you had problems with any students this year?"

"Nothing serious. Of course, there are always the ones who think it's my fault they're failing when they are the ones not turning in their homework."

"Have you had to reprimand anyone?"

"Sure. Don't we all? But no one stands out in my mind."

He pushed back from his desk and stood. "I'll pass this on to Ms. Porter and Carter, but short of giving this kid what he wants, I don't see what more we can do."

She stood. "How about we expel his sorry self."

"Believe me, if we figure out who it is, that will happen. In the meantime, please be vigilant about your surroundings, and if anyone makes you uncomfortable, remove yourself from the situation. If you ever need someone to talk to, you're welcome to give me a call anytime."

A hesitant look rested on her pretty face. His heart hurt for her and the situation she'd been thrust into. It wasn't fair of anyone to target her. Was he doing all he could? The entries he'd insisted on judging still awaited his attention. He should work on them tonight, but from the look on Anna's face she needed a friend more. "Are you doing anything tonight?"

She shrugged. "Why?"

The answer struck him. "Thought we could judge the contest entries together. It might make the time move faster."

She chuckled. "I could be persuaded to do that. Too much for you?" Her brows rose.

He snorted. "Ha. No, but I would enjoy the company."

Her eyes sparkled. "Sure. My place or yours?"

His brain blanked. What had he been thinking? He couldn't go to her place or she to his without causing the rumor mill to speculate about them. Anna had enough to deal with. "What about a neutral location?"

"Like a restaurant?"

That could be even worse. But at least they'd be in full view of anyone who cared to watch them, and it would be clear they were working. "Yes. How about Little Italy? It's quiet there, and the food is amazing."

"I haven't been. Sounds like a great idea, but will they mind us sitting there for a few hours tying up a table?"

"Hmm. I suppose that could be a problem. I'll figure out a place and text you."

"Works for me. See you later." She left with a little bounce to her step.

He locked up and exited via a side door near the school gym. A boy wearing a ball cap turned when he stepped outside. "Hi. You're Zander, right? How's it going?" He wasn't the senior's guidance counselor, but the guy was well known and one of the "popular" kids.

The young man turned. "Fine."

"You waiting for someone?"

"Yeah." He stuffed his hands into his jeans pockets.

"Okay." It wasn't odd for the students to hang out on campus after school, but the location was unusual. However, Zander wasn't breaking any rules, so he continued on to his car.

A scream ripped through the air. Titus raced toward the sound. Anna stood beside her car with tears streaming down her face and a photo in her hand. He raced to her side. "What's wrong?"

She thrust the picture at him. "If anyone hurt my Freddy..." her voice caught.

The photo was of her dog with a hand drawn picture of a knife at his throat and a message. "If you take away my love, I'll take away yours." He let out a puff of air. "This person crossed the line."

"You think?" She swiped at her face with a shaky hand.

"Let me take you home, and you can get Freddy. Then we'll go to the police station together and show them this." Anna was in no condition to drive, nor did he want to leave her alone. What did this kid hope to gain from threatening her like this? Especially since she had no idea who was behind it. It wasn't like hurting her or her dog would change anything.

Anna hadn't moved. He rested a hand at her elbow. "Come on. We can take my truck."

She nodded and walked beside him. "I'm freaking out, and I don't like freaking out." Anger filled her voice.

"I understand. If someone threatened Rudy like that I'd go ballistic."

"What if it was more than a threat?" She grabbed his arm. "We need to hurry." She looked around the parking lot. "Where's your truck?"

"It's over by the gym. We're almost there." They rounded the side of the building. Zander was nowhere to be seen. Why hadn't he come running too when Anna had screamed? At the very least he should have been surprised. Then again, Zander was all about Zander from what he'd observed.

Isaac Bugler, another senior, walked out the side door. Concern filled his face. "Is everything okay, Miss Plum? Someone said you were screaming in the parking lot."

"Everything is fine," Titus said. Poor Anna. He hadn't realized so many students were still in and around the school to witness her hysteria. He pulled his key from his pocket and clicked the remote to unlock the door.

Anna climbed into the front seat without saying a word, but she was visibly shaking.

He got behind the wheel and started the engine. "I'm sure Freddy is fine, Anna."

"This kid is sick in the head. It's one thing to mess with the contest entries and infect my computer with a worm. But to threaten my dog is sadistic."

"Yeah." He reached across the seat and grasped her hand. "I'm really sorry you're going through this. May I pray for you?"

She blinked then nodded and bowed her head.

"Lord, my friend here is hurting and scared for her beloved pet. Please take care of Freddy and protect him. And give Anna peace. Thank you. Amen." He released her hand.

"Thanks. I feel better already, but please hurry."

He did his best to stay only five miles above the speed limit while following Anna's instructions to her house. A few minutes later he parked on the street in front of her place.

She flung off the seatbelt and ran to the door.

Titus jogged after her and stopped in the doorway. Anna sat on the floor a few feet inside with Freddy in her lap licking a tear from her face. His throat thickened, and he blinked rapidly.

She looked up at him, smiling. "He's fine. I'll get his leash, and then we can go to the police station."

He nodded and cleared his throat. "Freddy looks happy to see you."

"He always is, but normally if I'd left the front door open, he would have taken off." She wrapped her arms around her dog and stood.

"He must have sensed your worry and wanted to reassure you."

"It's possible." She grabbed the leash from a hook beside the door. They walked back to his pickup. Somehow, she managed to climb into the cab with her dog in her arms. Clearly, she wasn't letting him go anytime soon.

Anna sat at her kitchen table across from Titus. His presence had a calming effect she desperately needed. After what had happened this afternoon, she was not leaving Freddy at home alone, so their dinner plans were altered. Instead of eating out, she'd thrown together a taco salad and picked up pie and ice cream from the grocery store. So much for warding off the town gossip he was so worried about. Maybe no one would notice his truck parked outside her house.

Titus looked up from his laptop. "I could use a break. How about that dessert you promised?"

She stretched and stifled a yawn. "Great idea. My brain is tired." She glanced at the clock on the microwave. "We've been at this for close to two hours." She stood and pulled out the vanilla ice cream and the berry pie.

"I believe it. My eyes ache." He stood and leaned against the counter. "How are you doing after what happened this afternoon?"

"I'm over the trauma, but to be honest, I'm angry that someone would go to such lengths to punish me for some perceived slight."

"So you think they were trying to punish you?"

"Yes. Don't you? What else could their intent have been?"

Titus shrugged. "I assumed they were attempting to blackmail you into making their entry score the highest and thereby win the contest."

"I could only do that if I knew who was behind this." She shook her head. "I think not being a finalist in the contest sent a fragile mind over the top. No matter what I do at this point, it's not going to matter. I'm going to push for a change in how the contest is handled too—no more blind entries. Someone needs to know who those entry numbers match up to. Working completely on a number system and expecting the students to save their entry form and assigned number is risky at best."

"Yes, but..."

She cut two slices of pie and placed them in the microwave to warm. "I suppose when something as valuable as a five-thousand-dollar scholarship is at stake, the students are extra careful. I guess I see why no one has had a problem providing proof of their entry number when the winner is announced."

"The blind entry format is fantastic and has worked well up to this year from what I've been told." Titus reached for the ice cream scooper.

"Your point?" she asked, sincerely curious.

"Only that the system has worked. I'm not sure it's wise to change it because of a single incident."

The microwave beeped. She pulled out the bowls and handed them to Titus for the ice cream. He might be right about the contest, but she'd always thought it was a strange way to do things. On the other hand, each story was judged on its own merit without prejudice.

Titus carried the bowls back to the table and sat. "I only have one more submission to judge. How about you?"

"Same. I would love to finish up tonight. I can't wait to be done with this contest."

"Me too. But I can't help wondering how everything will play out. When will this kid realize his threats were pointless?"

Anna gasped and jerked her chin up. "What if the kid's submission ends up being a finalist?"

"That would stink, considering the threats. But there's nothing to be done about it. If it happens though, and we can prove he or she was behind the trouble, I will do everything possible to make sure they don't receive any prize money."

A knock on her front door made Anna jump. Freddy started barking and charged toward the door. "Excuse me." She looked through the peephole then pulled open the door. "Hi, Nancy. Is everything okay?"

"I was going to ask you the same thing. I heard about Freddy." Nancy looked down at the dancing dog. "He's fine. What a relief."

"Come in."

"Thanks, but you have company." She waved toward Titus, who still sat at the kitchen table.

"Okay, but I'm curious why you thought Freddy wouldn't be okay. I assume you know what happened from Carter, and he knows my dog is fine."

Nancy frowned. "I didn't hear anything from Carter. Some kids I don't know were in the library talking about it."

A chair scraped on the floor, and a moment later Titus was by Anna's side. "How did they hear? No one knew but the police."

Her heart kicked into double time. This nightmare might finally be over.

Chapter Ten

NANCY OPENED HER LAPTOP ON ANNA'S kitchen table as she, along with Titus, hovered nearby. "It will take a minute for me to access the library's surveillance video from today."

"I think Nancy is trying to tell us to get back to work," Titus said.

"Who can work when we might have solved this mystery?" Anna shook her head. "Sorry. I'm done judging tonight."

Titus chuckled.

"Shh. At least go finish your dessert in the other room. Your hovering makes me nervous." She pulled up the feed from the library while the couple slunk away. Maybe she'd been too hard on them, but they really were making it difficult to think. It would take a chainsaw to cut through their tension.

The recording started at midnight. She skipped through to the two o'clock hour then pressed play. The students hadn't been discrete, so it should be easy enough to recognize them.

She focused on the screen, half-listening to the conversation in the other room. It sounded like Anna and Titus had bonded over this whole misadventure. The kids came onto the screen. Nancy clicked pause. "Here they are."

Anna and Titus rushed back into the room. Anna squatted on one side of Nancy while Titus hovered over her shoulder.

"Do you recognize them?" Nancy tilted her head to the side.

"Yes." They said in unison.

Nancy chuckled. "Then my work here is done."

"I'll pull them out and talk with each of them tomorrow," Titus said.

Anna stood then sank onto the nearest chair, her face in a daze.

"What's wrong? Aren't you excited?" Nancy figured Anna would be celebrating.

"No. I'm not. Those are two of my best students. I really like them. For some reason I figured the kid or kids behind this would be troublemakers. Not girls I considered trustworthy. One of them is my aid."

"That list you made stated the suspects would be good students," Nancy said.

Anna's gaze met hers. "I know, but why'd I have to be right?"

Nancy frowned. The elation of a moment ago fizzled. "You really like these kids." It wasn't a question. Anna was clearly devastated to have been betrayed by them. "I'm sorry you're hurting, but at least you know who is behind all of the threats."

"I suppose." Her pain-filled eyes tore at Nancy. She shifted her gaze to Titus. Based on the tender look in his eyes, he understood Anna needed some TLC. Nancy stood and spoke softly near his ear. "You got this?"

He nodded.

"I'll come back for my computer later." Nancy slipped from the house, and rather than go home, she set out on a walk. It wasn't fair what Anna was going through. Her friend knew the pain of betrayal from someone she'd cared about in the past, all too well. Would this throw her into a tailspin?

Nancy pumped her arms as she power-walked up the street toward the downtown district. As sad as she was for her friend, she was even more upset that Carter hadn't told her about the picture of Freddy. She'd assumed he hadn't known, but now she knew differently.

When would Carter have enough faith in her to tell her everything? Sure, it was sweet that he wanted to protect her from possible danger, and she should probably appreciate that he cared, but the fact was, she was annoyed. She really liked Carter, and yes, loved him too—at least she thought it was love—but if it were true love, would she be having second thoughts about their relationship?

A car slowed along the curb beside her. She looked at the driver. "Mom? What are you doing?"

"I was going to ask you the same. Don't you usually walk earlier in the evening? It's getting dark."

Nancy sighed. "I needed to walk and ponder. You know it's my best thinking time."

Mom stopped the car and got out. She leaned against the door. "Two minds work better than one. What are you trying to figure out?"

Nancy crossed her arms. "Thanks, but I need to figure this out on my own."

"Okay. How about a sounding board?"

"You're not going to take no for an answer, are you?" She shook her head. "Mom, sometimes thinking something through on my own is good. It builds character."

"So does trusting someone enough to let them in."

Nancy blew out a breath. "Good point. Lock up and walk with me. It's too cool out here to stand still." As she walked she explained her frustration and gradually relaxed. She hated that her mom was right about needing to talk—she really had needed someone to confide her frustrations to. She would have preferred Pepper, but Mom was good at listening.

"Have you told Carter how you're feeling?"

"No, and I don't plan to." How was she supposed to do that?

"The thing is, when two people are in a relationship, romantic or otherwise, communication is key. How would you feel if the situation was reversed? What if Carter came to you and said 'you don't support my passion so I want to break up'?"

"I'd feel blindsided and angry. But my situation is different. He knows helping people solve mysteries is my passion."

"True, but does he realize his protective nature is causing a rift to develop between the two of you?"

Nancy shrugged. She'd never said as much. "Shouldn't it go without saying?"

Mom laughed. "No. You can't expect a man to think the same way we do. If there's one thing I've learned in my position as the sheriff of Tipton County, it's that men and women approach things differently. I'm not saying one way is better than the other, only that we often see the world through a different lens."

"I hadn't considered..." Was she doing to Carter what he was to her by asking him to set aside his protective nature? "I see where you're going with this. And now more than ever I feel I must break things off with him."

"What?" Shock filled her mom's voice. "How did you come to that conclusion from this conversation?"

"It's simple. If I expect Carter to respect my passion and keep me in the loop for Anna's case, then I must respect his protective nature and not get upset when he tries to shield me from things."

"So your only conclusion is to break up? What about compromise? Or coming to an understanding? Is breaking up with Carter what you really want?"

"Of course not, but I love him too much to force him to change just to make me happy."

"It's times like these I wish you had a dad in your life."

"Ah, Mom." Nancy wrapped her arm around her mother and gave her a squeeze. Mom's ponytail brushed her arm. "You're all the parent I need. You're the best. I'll figure this out. And I promise not to do anything rash."

"Good. I'll be praying for both of you, and I encourage you to do the same. The Lord will help you with this if you'll let Him."

Nancy tilted her head toward her mom. "Thanks for the reminder. It's funny, I seldom think to bother Him with stuff."

"I guarantee you are not a bother."

"How can you say that?" Nancy knew the Lord loved her, but did He really care about her love life?

"I'm your mother. If I'm not bothered by helping you deal with things that concern you, why would your heavenly father be? He is capable of a love far greater than mine. He is the author of love. Goodness, now that I think about it, He's exactly who you should be talking to about this."

"Maybe you're right. I never thought about it like that before." Granted she'd never been in love before either.

The following morning Nancy caught herself pacing the library. She needed to settle down before Tara wondered what was up. She glanced toward the stacks where her assistant watched her—caught.

Tara laughed. "I wondered when you'd realize what you were doing."

Nancy glanced past her shoulder then gave the library a quick once over—they were alone. "I can't help it. I'm anxious about something."

"Wearing out the floor isn't going to help."

"I don't know, it might." She grinned.

Tara chuckled. "Since we're alone and things are slow, there's something I need to tell you."

"Oh? Something good, I hope." She was in knots already. She didn't need more to worry about. Waiting to hear from Anna or Titus was tough. She'd thought for sure one of them would have let her know how things had gone with the girls Titus was going to question.

"Well," Tara drew the word out. "That depends on you."

Uh-oh. "Maybe we'd better sit." Nancy pulled out a chair from a nearby table and dropped onto it.

Tara joined her then folded her hands atop the table. "Do you remember not long ago when a few books went missing?"

"Of course. Who could forget something like that? It's not every day I find original poetry left in place of a book. But what's this have to do with anything?"

"The thing is, I know how you enjoy solving a mystery."

Nancy nodded.

"You had been moping around this place for months, and I wanted to cheer you up, so I gave you a mystery to solve."

A slow grin spread on Nancy's face. "You're the bad poet?"

Tara nodded slowly. "Guilty. I still have the books, but I figured we were getting rid of them anyway, so it wouldn't matter."

"That was sweet of you. Why'd you stop, since I never figured out who had done it?"

"There was no need. Once all this trouble started at the school with your friend, you were back to your usual self again. To be honest, I hadn't planned to confess, but my conscience has been eating at me." Tara looked down then back at Nancy. "Am I in trouble?"

"For trying to get me out of my funk—which you did, by the way. Not a chance. I could never fire someone who looks out for me like you do." She gasped. If she wouldn't fire Tara for looking out for her, why would she dump Carter for doing the same?

Nancy bolted to her feet. "Can you handle things here for a while? I need to go do something."

"Sure. Keep your ringer on though, in case I need you."

"I will." She grabbed her purse and rushed

outside into the cool spring air. She'd done as her mom had suggested and asked the Lord for direction regarding Carter. The Lord had been quiet, but she knew without doubt He'd orchestrated this conversation with Tara.

Chapter Eleven

TITUS WAITED UNTIL ANNA'S PREP PERIOD to call each of the girls into his office. They both sat on seats in the waiting area. He stood and walked to the doorway. "Valerie, will you come in please? Autumn, I'll be with you shortly." He returned to his desk chair.

Valerie walked in, an uneasy look covering her face.

"Please close the door and have a seat." Each of the counselors' offices had a window wall that looked out into the waiting area so anyone could look in, but so long as he spoke quietly, no one outside would hear their conversation.

"What's going on Mr. Gains? Is this about graduation? I pulled my grade up in Algebra Two to a C, but my parents are furious that I have a C since I've always been an A student."

"I can see why that would concern them. Is there something going on that's causing you to do poorly in that class?"

"Other than the teacher doesn't teach? Not really. Math has always been my hardest subject."

He'd heard similar statements from other students about this particular teacher, but since he didn't make a habit of checking student grades, he'd had no idea Valerie was struggling. "I wish you would have come to me. I might have been able to move you to another class."

Her eyes widened. "I didn't think of it. I've never had to change classes because of a teacher."

He nodded, wondering at the direction their conversation had taken. Valerie didn't fit the profile of the person they were looking for, but the evidence said differently. He cleared his throat. "I'll do whatever I can to help with this math situation, but that's not why you're here. I'd like to talk with you about the picture of Miss Plum's dog."

She frowned. "O-kay," she drew out the word.

"Who took it?"

"I don't know."

"Then how'd you get it?"

"I didn't. I never saw it."

"I'm confused. You were overheard talking about the photo."

"So? That doesn't mean I took it."

"How'd you know about it?"

"Autumn told me."

He glanced out the window to where the other senior waited. Her knee bounced as she messed around on her phone. Anna had shared she'd hoped the instigator was Valerie and not Autumn since Autumn was her aid. This development was going to be a kick in the gut. He hurt for Anna and wanted to take her pain away, but the best he could do was reprimand the student.

"Is Autumn in trouble?"

"Thanks for your help. You may return to class now."

"But—"

"We're done for now." He stood and followed her to the door. The girl clearly wanted to know more, but no matter how he replied it would only create more questions. "Autumn, please come in and put your phone away."

She did as he asked and sat. "Is everything okay?"

"I'm afraid not. You were overheard discussing a photo of Miss Plum's dog."

"Oh, yeah. That was so mean. Is her dog okay?"

Titus studied the brunette. Her brown eyes appeared sincere and her body language no longer looked nervous. "Yes. He's fine, but we're concerned for his continued safety."

"Yeah. That's messed up." Her eyes widened. "You think *I* sent that picture?"

"It crossed my mind." Although, he was having second thoughts. Autumn was either an exceptional actress or she was as clueless as she appeared.

"I would never. Miss Plum is awesome. I'm her T.A." Her gaze slammed into his. "Does she think I did that? Oh no!" She stood and rushed to the door.

"Autumn, sit! We aren't finished here."

Her eyes watered. "But Miss Plum has to know the truth. I would never do anything like that. No wonder she seemed upset today."

"You can see her after school. Now please take a seat."

Shoulders slumped, she returned to the chair and sat. "Why can't I go now?"

"Because I need your help. Do you have any idea who is behind the photo and the threat?"

"Actually, I never saw it. I overheard a couple of guys talking. They were laughing about it."

"Who were they?"

"I didn't see their faces. I only saw them from

behind, and they kind of scared me, so I turned around and went out another door."

He blew out the breath he hadn't realized he was holding. "I see. I'd appreciate you keeping this conversation to yourself. You can tell your parents, but I'd rather other students not get wind of this."

"I won't say a word. If those guys find out I overheard them..." She shivered. "They really gave me the creeps."

"So you didn't recognize their voices or anything? The school isn't that big. Surely they at least sounded familiar."

"I wish. I think they might have been underclassmen."

"Oh." He'd assumed they'd be juniors or seniors. "Okay. Thanks, Autumn. If you hear anything, please let me know. We'd really like to make sure Miss Plum's dog isn't in any danger."

She nodded. "I will for sure. Are we done now?"

"Yes, you may return to class." He sat back and tapped a pen against his desk. Two dead ends. He dialed Anna's classroom. "Hi, do you have a minute to meet me in my office?"

"I'll be right there." Before he even had time to collect his thoughts Anna was in his office. "What do you know?"

"Come in and close the door." After she seated herself, he told her everything.

"I don't know how to feel. I'm happy Autumn and Valerie weren't involved, but whoever did it is still unknown."

"Yes. And that's a problem. Where's Freddy today?"

"I locked his doggie door so he couldn't get into the backyard. I hope he doesn't destroy my house though."

"Do you have anyone who can go check on him and let him out for a bit?"

She shook her head.

A tap sounded on the glass. He grinned. "Look who's here." He motioned to Nancy to come in.

"Hey, there. Any news?" Nancy stood inside the threshold to his office. "I stopped by the sheriff's department, and thought I'd swing by here to see what the girls said."

Titus stood and brought another chair into his office.

Nancy sat. "Thanks." She looked at Anna then him. "Is the case of the sore loser solved?"

Anna shook her head. "Not even close. The girls didn't have anything to do with it."

Titus filled her in on what he'd learned.

"Sounds like a good news, bad news kind of day. Sweet junipers, that frosts me. I thought this would be over."

"Me too," Anna said. "Do you have time to run to my house and play with Freddy for a bit? I'm worried he's going to destroy something since he's locked inside all day."

"I can make time."

Relief shone on Anna's face. "Thank you. You have my spare key, right?"

"I do." Nancy stood. "We'll talk more later." She hustled out.

Titus stood. "I'll walk you back to your classroom."

"That's not necessary."

"I know. But I'd like to if it's all right."

"Sure." His thoughtfulness warmed her heart. He was truly a kind man.

They walked side by side through the nearly empty halls. A few students with bathroom passes were here and there. "I'd feel more comfortable if, while you're on campus, you always have a staff member with you until we catch the person behind the threats."

"Is that really needed?"

"No, but like I said, it'd make me more comfortable. I can't force you to do it, Anna. It's up to you, but I think it's wise counsel."

"I appreciate your concern, and I'll think about your suggestion."

"Good." He stopped outside her classroom door and waited as she unlocked it. He looked over his shoulder then back to Anna, lowering his voice. "I finished judging the entries you gave me. I'll email everything to you before the end of the day so you can re-post the results." And he'd be watching all the students very carefully as they read the results too.

Anna sat on the couch in Nancy's living room while Freddy chewed a bone at her feet. "I'm so nervous, I can hardly think straight. What if this kid comes after Freddy now that the results have been posted?"

"We will keep a close eye on Freddy."

"I don't want him locked up in the house every day while I'm at work. Thanks again for visiting him earlier. I'm sure that's the reason he didn't destroy my house."

Nancy chuckled. "He has more than his fair share of energy, but so long as someone walks him or plays with him, I think your house will be safe."

"Which means I need to find a dog walker." Her body temperature rose in sync with her temper. "Can you believe Titus asked me to not be alone on campus?"

Nancy frowned. "He must think you're in danger." She stood and paced to the window then spun around toward Anna. "When you posted the results of the contest this afternoon, did you pay attention to who checked the results?"

"Yes, but they're posted online as well." She couldn't get Nancy's statement out of her mind. Was she in danger? Would this kid actually hurt her, or was he making idle threats against her dog to manipulate her into giving him what he wanted? But if that was the case, she'd have to know who he was— he had to realize she was clueless. If that was all true, then what was this guy thinking? What was his motivation? Had she read the entire situation all wrong?

Nancy cringed. "I wish you hadn't done that. We could have narrowed our suspect pool dramatically with that information."

"Done what?" She'd been so lost in thought, she'd forgotten what they were talking about.

"Posted the results online. I'd hoped we'd be able to observe the students who checked the results."

Anna clenched her hands. "I didn't think of that. I'm not good at this like you are." Her entire body ached from the stress of it all.

Nancy waved a hand. "Don't beat yourself up. I should've said something."

"Thanks for trying to make me feel better." It hadn't worked, but she appreciated Nancy's thoughtfulness.

"My mom and I were talking about another matter, and she reminded me of something I often forget."

Nancy's reflective tone grabbed Anna's attention again. "What's that?"

"That the Lord loves us more than we can imagine, and He wants the best for us. She didn't use those exact words, but it's what stuck in my mind. I know He doesn't want harm to come to you or Freddy. We need to be praying the culprit is found and stopped before he does something stupid that can't be undone."

Anna blinked back tears. "You're right. I've been so caught up in the stress of this mess, I completely forgot to go to Him for help. Thank you for the reminder."

Nancy nodded.

"I should head home."

"Okay." Nancy walked with her to the door. "Does the high school have surveillance cameras?"

"Only in a few key places. Why?"

"I'm thinking we could view the footage to see who was in the hall near the gym as well as who all paid attention to the original contest posting and this one. I realize some students might have looked the results up online, but you never know."

Anna's heart skipped. "That's a great idea. I can't believe no one thought of that. I'll call Titus to see if he can arrange it." She scooped Freddy into her arms. "I'll let you know what he says. Would you like to join us when we watch the footage?"

"I'd love to." Nancy scratched Freddy's back. "You be a good boy for your mama."

He barked.

Anna jumped then laughed. "He said he promises to behave."

Nancy chuckled. "Oh, I'm sure that was it." She stepped outside with them.

"I'll call you when we have a plan." Anna hustled toward her house next door, noting that Nancy stayed on her porch until she got to her door. The woman was as bad as Titus. At least Luke had been available to walk her to her car this afternoon. There was no guarantee she'd be able to use the buddy system all the time, but she'd do her best. She couldn't deny the safety in numbers rule. After all, it was a motto she'd come to live by even before the recent events surrounding her.

After a quick call to Titus, she prepared a light meal for herself, then headed to the backyard. It was still a little cool, but Freddy needed time to run around. She sank into the padded aluminum chair.

Freddy charged after a squirrel that raced up the fence then disappeared on the other side.

"Good job, Freddy." She bit into the grilled cheese sandwich. Comfort food at its finest. Her doorbell rang. "That's odd. Be right back, boy." She rushed to answer the door and pulled it open. "Luke. This is a surprise." The look on his face shot fear through her. "What's wrong?"

Chapter Twelve

LUKE'S PULSE THRUMMED IN HIS EARS as he stood on Anna's front porch. He'd debated coming to her home without calling first, but she deserved to know what was going on and not via a phone call or text message. "May I come in?"

She stepped aside. "I have Freddy in the backyard. Do you mind if we sit out there?"

"No." At least she'd be sitting when he told her the news. If he'd known things were going to get turned upside down, he never would have insisted someone else do the contest. Then again, he was beginning to wonder if the contest was the root of the problem.

"Would you like something to drink?" She paused by the kitchen.

"No, thank you."

Worry creased her brow. "What brings you by?" Anna walked outside into the backyard and sat in a comfortable looking lawn chair. She motioned to an identical one beside it, facing the grassy yard. Her dog sniffed around bushes on the far side of the yard.

"There was a development late this afternoon that you need to know about. Someone filed an official complaint against you."

Her eyes bulged. "Why? Who?"

"I don't know much, but as the department head I was notified. I wanted to give you a heads-up before

Ms. Porter got to you tomorrow." He knew with all his being that the claim was false and felt for her. If only there was something he could do.

Her face paled. "I don't understand. What am I being investigated for?"

"Helping students cheat. Your accuser stated that you provide test answers to students."

"That's absurd! Why would I do that?"

"Based on all that has been transpiring, it's clear to me that someone is out to get you. I'm really sorry about this."

Anna gasped. "You know I'd never do something like that."

"I don't believe for a minute you're guilty. I will do everything in my power to make sure the administration knows too."

"I appreciate that."

If he'd had any doubt in his mind that there was a shred of truth to the allegations, Anna's response would have erased them. It was clear to him she was blindsided. He grasped her hand and gave it a quick squeeze then released it. "Everything will work itself out."

"I don't know how you can say that. Ever since I took over the writing contest my life has been turned topsy-turvy. Do you think my accuser is the same kid who's been causing me problems?"

"I don't know, but your accuser's identity is being withheld."

She stood and paced a few feet then back. "This kid is out to get me. It seems he will stop at nothing to do it, and the system is playing into his hand." She looked ready to pull her hair out, and he didn't blame her. She plopped back into the chair.

"I agree, but the question that bothers me is *why* this person is so bent on destroying you." He shifted to better face her and leaned forward. "Think, Anna. What has happened in the past month, besides the writing contest that would cause someone to attack you?"

She shook her head. "Nothing out of the ordinary except the contest."

"Okay then. Walk through the past month in your mind. What about the interactions you've had with students—no matter how innocent? Could one of them have misunderstood or been embarrassed by something you said?"

She blinked rapidly. "I don't know. You know how kids are. They hear what they want to hear." She took an unsteady breath. "Let me think."

He watched her face closely. Clearly, she was scared and frustrated. He didn't blame her. From what he could tell, her job was her life—her students her family.

What would she do if the allegations stuck? He wouldn't put it past this kid to plant evidence against Anna.

Her body stiffened as her panicked gaze slammed into his. "I'm stumped. I always try to be an encourager to my students. No incidents come to mind."

"Okay. Maybe sleep on it."

"How come I can't know who filed the complaint? If I knew, I'd be able to respond to the allegation better."

He blew out a breath. "School policy. I'm sorry.

But you should know that Ms. Porter seemed to think the accusation was unfounded."

"That's good." She wrapped her arms around her middle. "But this whole thing is absurd. I feel sick." Her voice caught.

He stood and squeezed her shoulder.

She reached up and rested her hand over his. "Thank you for caring enough to deliver this news in person so I wouldn't be blindsided at work tomorrow."

His nerve endings jolted at her touch. "If you need anything at all, please ask. I'm serious."

"I could really use a hug." She looked up at him with watery eyes.

His breath caught in his lungs. He slid his hand from under hers and opened his arms.

She stood and stepped close. He wrapped her in a bear hug and breathed in the lavender and vanilla scent of her hair. His heart raced. He hadn't held any woman but his wife since forever, and she'd been gone for years. He willed his pulse to slow.

Anna leaned back. "Thanks. I'm sorry if I made you feel uncomfortable."

He dropped his arms and took a step back. "Not at all." *Liar!* He'd always been overly empathetic. He felt sorry for her, that's all this was. Nothing more.

The sun dipped in the sky, and the lights edging Anna's flowerbeds had begun to glow. "I should head home before my little darling sneaks out."

Anna's eyes widened. "I didn't realize Maddie was still doing that."

He chuckled. "Not so much anymore. But I have a difficult time trusting her after what happened this past fall."

"I understand. She spends a lot of time with Gavin. They seem like best friends."

"They are. I keep a close eye on those two. It's refreshing to see they aren't romantically involved." He chuckled. "I actually asked her once if Gavin was her boyfriend."

"What'd she say?"

"After rolling her eyes, she told me that everyone asks them that, but they're just friends." He was thankful too. He wasn't ready for his little girl—well maybe not so little—to have a boyfriend.

"They would make a cute couple, but it's nice they are only friends. Before Gavin moved to town, Maddie was reserved and kept to herself."

"I think you've had a lot to do with her stepping out of her comfort zone as well. Asking her to co-lead the book club was brilliant."

Anna smiled. "Thanks."

Her eyes sparkled in spite of the bad news he'd delivered—breathtaking. He shook his head and looked away. Before he said anything stupid he headed for the gate then turned and waved. "Don't worry, Anna. God's got this. I'm sure you'll be cleared of this accusation in no time."

The next day, Anna stared out her living room window. She'd never been so happy to be home. Today had been so far past awkward it was ridiculous. Ms. Porter had sat in on all her classes after talking with her before school about the accusation—how did the woman have time to observe her *all day*? The worst part was her students had begun to notice that the principal spent the entire day in her classes— she'd seen one kid take a picture of her boss then post it online. She'd taken the phone away until class was out, but it was clear there'd be no hiding something was up.

How long until the entire school started gossiping about her? She couldn't even leave her house except to go to work, out of fear people would ask questions. If Ms. Porter planned to be in her class again tomorrow, Anna might go home sick. It wasn't far from the truth either—this whole thing had taken a toll on her.

She couldn't sleep last night, and her body was a ball of knots. *Lord, I need a miracle. Please stop whoever is out to destroy me. And please help me to stay strong in You. Dealing with this kid is proving to be one of the hardest things I've ever faced.* Anna closed her eyes as tears seeped out and slid down her face.

Freddy nudged her leg and barked.

"What is it, boy?"

He danced in a circle and barked again.

She wiped her eyes. "You want to play? Let's go to the backyard." She grabbed an old tennis ball and headed toward the door. Freddy raced ahead and leaped through his doggie door. She frowned. Hadn't she locked that thing? She slid the people door open and stepped out. A light drizzle dropped from gray clouds. Hopefully Freddy wouldn't get too dirty.

She tossed the ball and laughed as he slid on the damp grass. He raced back to her and dropped the ball at her feet. She lobbed it this time. He charged after it, scooped it up in his mouth, and raced around the perimeter of the yard following the trail he'd embedded into the grass. It looked like he was done with her for now.

"Come, Freddy." She wasn't about to leave him alone out here where someone bent on destroying her life could get to him.

Her dog trotted back inside through his door. She stepped inside too, then locked both doors—Freddy's and the slider. She might be paranoid, but no one was going to hurt her dog.

She looked around her house and noted dust and dog hair. Cleaning always relaxed her—she grabbed a dusting cloth and got to work.

By late afternoon, the house was as clean as it had ever been, and her arms were sore. At least the day hadn't been a complete waste. She headed for the bathroom, flipped on the overhead fan, and ran the water for the shower.

She closed her eyes and let the water pound her tired muscles. How long she stood under the hot streaming water she had no idea. Unfortunately, she couldn't wash away what was going on at work like she could wash away the dust in her hair. She finally turned off the water and stepped out. The bathroom felt like a sauna.

It sounded as though her exhaust fan needed to be replaced—no surprise really, considering the horrible racket it made. The motor was so old and loud it could be heard throughout the house.

She quickly got dressed. The scent of her soap lingered in the air as she towel-dried her hair. She should probably blow it dry but didn't have the energy. Instead, she wove it into a French braid and called it good.

Freddy plopped down in the doorway to the bathroom and gazed up at her with pleading eyes.

"What are you looking at?" She grinned. "I know you're hungry, but you're going to have to wait until I'm done in here. I'll be quick." Five minutes later, satisfied with her appearance, Anna fed Freddy then took him to the backyard for more playtime.

She tossed his ball several times and laughed as he rolled to a stop at the far end of the yard. "Come on, Freddy. Let's go." She clapped her hands, getting his attention. He raced inside ahead of her.

A pickup rolled to a stop in front of her house. *Titus.* Her stomach leapt—did he have news? A moment later he headed up to her front door. Her pulse tripped then raced. She pulled it open before he could knock. "Hi."

"Mind if I come in?"

"Please." She opened the door wider and stepped aside. "Have a seat."

Freddy yapped and danced in a circle. Chuckling, Titus squatted to scratch her dog's back. "I wanted to see how you're doing. Luke filled me in on what's going on."

Her entire body heated. "Does everyone know? Maybe I'll pretend to be sick tomorrow—although that's not much of a stretch."

He frowned. "I don't think anyone but those who need to know are aware of your situation."

"Good." She sank into the easy chair facing the couch where Titus sat. Her tension eased ever so slightly, but it was little relief.

"I'd ask how you're doing, but based on your comment, I'd say not well."

"I've been better." He didn't need to know she couldn't sleep or eat.

"Your house looks spotless."

"Thanks. I clean when I'm upset." She chuckled humorlessly. "At this rate, I'll have the cleanest house in town. I wonder how long it will take to have my name cleared."

He shrugged. "I wish I knew. Does Nancy know what's going on?"

She shook her head. "It's so humiliating. I know it's impossible to expect it, but I don't want anyone to know." She understood why Luke told Titus but wished he hadn't.

"Nancy would want to help. Plus, you shouldn't be alone with your thoughts."

Her heart warmed at his concern. "That's sweet, but I think I'd prefer that, than face anyone right now."

"That's your pride talking. You know what they say about pride."

She sighed. "Yes. Pride goes before a fall. I can't go much lower than I am now though." Unless someone else lied about her, and she was found guilty of helping students cheat. Her stomach churned.

"Things could get worse before they get better. We must figure out who is behind all your trouble. Luke and I know you personally and believe without a doubt the allegation is false, but you have to be proven innocent to clear your name."

"You're not helping me feel any better," she said drily.

To his credit he looked remorseful. "I suppose not. I know my timing could be better, but would you like to go out sometime?"

Her heart tripped. "I...yes?" His timing was better than he realized. She needed the diversion.

He chuckled. "Was that a question?"

Like a battering ram, reality slammed into her, reminding her why he was here and the likely reason he asked her out—he felt sorry for her. She wasn't a charity case. "With all that's going on, I'm afraid to be seen in public outside of school. The kids were shooting off messages to one another like crazy by the end of the day. I sure wish Ms. Porter hadn't been so obvious about observing my classes. Besides, I've heard dating a co-worker is a bad idea."

He grinned. "That's probably true, but it might turn out to be a great idea." He raised a brow. "I don't mind being a distraction for you. We could drive to Salem. Go see a movie or dinner or both. Whatever you'd like."

Had she misread the motivation behind him asking her out? He seemed sincere—even interested. "Maybe we could go for a walk in one of the parks."

"Now that's a great idea! See what I mean?"

She laughed. "Thank you."

"For what?"

"Making me laugh. I needed that."

His face softened. "Anytime. What are your plans for the rest of today? I have an idea that might intrigue you."

"Do tell." She couldn't stop smiling, which was nuts, since aside from the day she was jilted at the altar, the past forty-eight hours had been the worst of her life.

Chapter Thirteen

THE DAY AFTER HE'D BROKEN THE news about the cheating accusation, Luke knocked at Anna's door. Freddy barked wildly on the other side. If Anna were home, surely she would have answered by now. Where was she? He'd told her he'd be stopping by when he'd passed her in the hall at school today. Was she avoiding him? And if so, why?

He could always call or text her, but he'd rather talk to her in person—he didn't want an electronic trail of his contact with her. He'd been told in no uncertain terms from their boss that he wasn't allowed to have any contact with Anna while the investigation was in progress—absurd and unprecedented. He'd protested, but his boss was adamant. Had she discovered something he'd missed? No way. He believed with his entire being that Anna was innocent.

He turned to leave and startled when a snap sounded. He looked around Anna's yard but didn't see any damaged trees or anyone lurking. Shaking his head, he headed for his car. A cat must have snapped a twig.

"Dad?" Maddie stopped at the bottom of Anna's driveway with Gavin by her side. "What are you doing?"

"Nothing. How about you?"

"We were coming to see Miss Plum. We were

supposed to have a book club meeting this afternoon, but she didn't show."

That couldn't be good. There was definitely more going on than he realized. "Miss Plum isn't answering her door. Tell you what, if that ever happens again, come and find me. I'll sit in for her."

"*You?*" Maddie's mouth hung open.

He chuckled. "Better close that before a bug flies in."

She pressed her lips together.

Gavin crossed his arms. "Why wasn't Miss Plum there? She's never missed a meeting."

He sighed. Walking toward the kids he motioned for them to get into his car. "She's going through a rough patch right now. You want a ride home, Gavin?"

"Sure. Thanks."

The kids scrambled into his car. His eyes met Gavin's in the rearview mirror as he pulled away from the curb. "You both know that someone from the school is harassing Miss Plum."

They nodded.

"Between us, I believe this same person has filed an official complaint stating that Miss Plum has been helping students cheat."

"That's horrible!" Maddie said. "No way would she do that. Miss Plum is honest." Maddie crossed her arms. "Gavin and I have her, and we would know if that was true. I feel sorry for her."

His daughter's passion didn't surprise him. She'd always been like that, even as a toddler. "I'm sure she appreciates your support, but please don't let on that you know about the cheating thing. I probably shouldn't have told either of you, but I thought you might have heard kids talking at school."

"Nope." Gavin shook his head. "Kids rarely talk bad about Miss Plum, because she's great. She's tough, but she cares about us. Makes me work even harder in her class than I do in the rest."

Gavin sighed. "Now I really wish I knew who I overheard talking about her in the locker room. We need to figure this out before her reputation goes down the toilet. I know you and my uncle said Maddie and I need to stay out of it, but I really think we could help without getting involved."

"How so?" Luke had a lot of respect and admiration for Anna, and at this point, he was willing to hear Gavin out for Anna's sake.

"All we need to do is listen to what's going on around us. We wouldn't even need to ask anyone what they know."

"Yeah, Dad. Please let us help."

"I'm proud of you both for your willingness to help your teacher, Gavin, but you need to talk to your uncle. As for Maddie," he glanced her way, "I think I spoke too soon the other day—things have gotten worse, and I'd welcome any information you overhear. Miss Plum's career could be destroyed if we don't find this kid."

"I'll ask my uncle tonight. Don't forget to stop." He pointed to the driveway one house ahead.

"Right." He'd almost driven past the boy's house. He hit the brake hard as he signaled and pulled over. "Would you like to come over for dinner tonight?"

"Really?" Excitement bubbled in the boy's voice.

"Sure. Maddie's at your place all the time. The weather is nice enough, so I can grill burgers. You interested?"

"Yeah. Thanks. But I have to check with my uncle." Gavin got out. "Text me the time, and I'll let you know." He jogged up to his front door then turned and waved.

"I like your friend," Luke said as he drove away.

"Thanks. He's great. I don't know how I survived before he moved here."

Luke had a pretty good idea. From what he understood, Maddie had been up to mischief every night after he'd gone to bed. Apparently, it was her way of dealing with his neglect and her mother's death. Would he ever be able to forgive himself for making her feel unloved and unwanted?

He knew the Lord forgave him, but forgiving himself was hard, especially since he didn't want to make the same mistake again. "Maddie?"

"Hmm?"

"Do you have any idea why this person would target Miss Plum?"

"No, but I thought it had to do with the writing contest." Confusion laced her voice.

"We think it does, but to be honest, we don't know anything for sure. How do the kids at school feel about her?"

"Like Gavin said, she's well liked. I suppose she makes someone angry from time to time, but most of us get mad at our teachers every so often."

He nodded. "I guess."

"What time should Gavin come over?" She held her phone with her thumbs poised over the screen. "His uncle said it was fine."

"We'll eat by six, but he can come over before

that."

She focused on her phone. "Thanks, Dad."

"Sure thing. Maybe next week you could ask a girl over."

She laughed. "Yeah, right. You know I don't have any girlfriends."

He didn't actually, but sadly the news wasn't shocking. "Okay."

He felt her gaze on him as he pulled into their driveway and put the car in park. He looked her way. "What?"

"You're different."

"Good or bad?"

"Good."

"I'm trying." He turned off the car and got out.

"Race you to the door." She jetted ahead of him. He charged after her losing by only two steps. "Ha! Beat you." She frowned. "What's this?" She pulled an envelope from the crack of the door.

Dread hit him.

Nancy headed outside for her powerwalk and to meet up with Anna, but she spotted her hopping into Titus's pickup instead. It looked as though her friend stood her up—odd. Nancy's phone chimed for an incoming text message.

Going out with Titus for dinner. Have to miss our walk. Ttyl.

Talk to you later. Hmm.

You go, girl. I want all the details. Call as late as you want or come over.

She pressed send and pocketed her phone. A

giggle escaped her lips. She was so happy for Anna. She knew those two would hit it off. She set out at an easy pace.

Five minutes into her walk, a sheriff's cruiser pulled up alongside her. Nancy looked at the driver and waved to Lyle. He lowered the passenger window. "Long time, no see."

"What's up?" She squatted beside the vehicle.

"Keeping an eye out for trouble—the usual."

"The graffiti artist is still at large?" She knew the answer but hoped he might give her some inside information that Carter hadn't.

"I'm afraid so, but to be honest, he or she isn't much of a priority. It only happened the one time."

"At multiple houses that mostly belonged to high school English teachers. You don't think that's odd?"

"Sure it is, but it's not a priority. If the vandalism had continued, that'd be different. As it stands, nothing further has happened."

"Yet." She stood, too annoyed to be friendly. Her mom and Carter should know better than to make assumptions rather than consider all possibilities. What was going on with the sheriff's department?

"I recognize that fire in your eyes," Lyle said. "Simmer down. There are things you don't know."

She blew a piece of hair out of her eyes. "Figures. It was nice to see you, Lyle. Don't be a stranger. You and my mom should come over for dinner some time." Now why had she said that? Based on the look of surprise on Lyle's face, he wondered the same. "To talk shop, of course."

He chuckled. "You never give up. See you." He signaled and pulled away.

"Never." With renewed determination to figure out who was behind the graffiti and Anna's torment, Nancy continued on her walk, pondering what Lyle was saying without saying it. He was patrolling the street, but the graffiti artist wasn't a priority. The commander could usually be found behind a desk, not the steering wheel of a patrol car—something was definitely up.

A girl riding her bike toward Nancy stopped. "Hi. Remember me? I'm Lauren. We met in Mr. Harms's class."

"Of course. How are you? Have you been by the library yet?" Contrary to popular belief, Nancy had a life and didn't work, eat, and sleep within the walls of her favorite place in town.

"No. But the summer reading program sounds fun. You'll probably see me there after school lets out for the summer."

"Great. I look forward to it. We have a wonderful young adult section."

Lauren tilted her head, and a shy look covered her face. "Actually, I prefer Christian romance."

"Then you won't be disappointed. But why do you look embarrassed about that?"

"Sometimes when I tell people what I like to read, they make fun of me. Especially since I read romance."

Nancy frowned. "I don't understand. Why would they make fun of you?"

"They say only girls without boyfriends like romance books." Her face tinged pink.

"Shows how much they know. Take it from me, lots of people, single, married, or in a relationship enjoy romance novels. It's a well-read genre. You can quote me on that."

Lauren grinned. "I will. Thanks, Miss Daley. It's rough being single. Girls like me need role models like you."

Nancy stifled a laugh. "Actually, I have a boyfriend, but I spent most of my life single."

"I broke up with my boyfriend not all that long ago. He was my first." A sad look engulfed her face.

"I'm sorry."

"It's fine. I broke up with him. He and I were too different."

"How so?"

"Oh, you know. I go to church, but he doesn't want anything to do with God. I won't sleep with him, so he called me a prude—that kind of thing. I really liked him, but what he wanted wasn't going to happen."

"That's mature of you. Good job standing up for your convictions."

"Thanks. When I told a teacher at school about him, she suggested we take a break from each other. Then I realized I wanted more than a break." An unreadable expression crossed Lauren's face. "I need to get home before my mom starts to worry."

"Okay. I hope to see you around."

"You will. Now that I know the library has Christian romance, I'll be there all the time. See you." She peddled away.

The world needed more young people like Lauren. What a great kid. Nancy set out again, pumping her arms as she walked. Her thoughts drifted back to her conversation with Lyle. Had he been trying to tell her something without saying it?

One thing was for certain, she needed to follow through with her dinner invitation, and she'd include Carter too. Thankfully they all worked the same shift right now, so it would be doable.

Her phone buzzed. She pulled it out of her pocket and answered. "I was just thinking about you."

"Good thoughts, I hope," Carter said.

Nancy grinned. "The best. I sort of invited Lyle and my mom for dinner, and I'd like you to come too."

"Sounds good to me. When?"

"I'm not sure yet. I'll get back to you on that. What's going on with you?"

"I wanted to hear your voice."

Her heart melted. "That's sweet. And now I don't want to share you with my mom and Lyle. How about you come over in a couple of hours? I'll throw something together for dinner." Thankfully she hadn't invited Lyle over for tonight. "I'll have all of you over another time."

"Just you and me? No shop talk?"

She heard the desire in his voice and slowed her pace. "If that's what you want. I promise no shop talk." It had been her intent to probe him for information about what Lyle was up to, but she needed to learn boundaries, and tonight would be good practice. In fact, it'd be a good time to put into practice some of those romantic dinners she'd read about and seen in Hallmark movies.

"Thanks. How does six o'clock work?"

"Fine. I'll see you then." That didn't give her as much time as she'd hoped for, but she'd make it work. She turned and headed home. The steaks in the freezer could thaw in the microwave in time to throw on the grill. She compiled a list of things from the grocery store she'd need to pick up—crusty bread, salad fixings, flowers, candles, and chocolate dipped strawberries for dessert.

A candlelit dinner—she grinned, and excitement shot through her at the thought of a romantic meal with only the two of them. Once back at her house she threw the steaks in the microwave then quickly showered. She yanked on a clean pair of sweats and a T-shirt, set the partially thawed steaks on the counter to come to room temperature, then headed out.

If everything went according to plan she'd have the time to race home, prepare the salad, set the table, and change into something fitting for a romantic dinner. Excitement bubbled in her as she backed out of her driveway and headed for the nearby grocery store. She hummed a praise tune she'd heard on the radio the other day. One green light after the other met her as she soared up Main Street.

A blur in her peripheral vision grabbed her attention. She turned her head and slammed on the brakes. Metal crushed metal. Her head whipped toward the driver's side window. Pain exploded. Everything went black.

"She's waking up. Get a doctor."

"Mom?" Nancy pried her eyes open. Bright light caused her to squint. "Where am I?"

"The hospital. You were T-boned."

"Right. I remember now." She winced and caught

her breath. Pain radiated from her neck and shoulders along with a pounding headache, and soreness held her whole body hostage. "What's wrong with me?"

The hospital door whooshed open, and a woman wearing a white coat followed by Carter walked into her room. The doctor smiled. "Welcome back. I'm Doctor Mercy. How are you feeling?"

"Like I was in a car accident." She caught Carter's gaze. The love and concern that shone in his eyes spiked her pulse.

The doctor chuckled, pulling Nancy's thoughts and attention back to her.

"Makes sense." She stood beside Nancy's bed and seemed to study one of the monitors—probably her pulse that was beating out of control. "How about specifically? Where do you hurt?"

"My head is pounding, and I hurt all over."

Dr. Mercy nodded then she shined a light into Nancy's eyes. "Your head is throbbing because you have a concussion. The good news is there doesn't appear to be any internal injuries, or broken bones. I'd like to keep you through the night, and barring any surprises, you should make a full recovery. I'll check back in with you tomorrow, and we'll talk about letting you go home."

It was on the tip of her tongue to argue, but she didn't have the energy. Her thoughts shot to her car— a classic blue Mustang. Dread washed over her. She loved that car.

The doctor gently patted her arm. "Get some rest." She left the room.

"You're quiet," her mom said. "I expected you to argue with the doctor."

"I don't feel good enough to argue. How's my car?" She looked to Carter and worried her bottom lip. The look on his face didn't bode well for her car. "Will someone please tell me?"

Mom's brow furrowed. "Likely totaled."

Nancy groaned. "Was the other driver drunk? Or what?"

"No. Two teens were racing. One stopped at the light, the other didn't."

"How's the driver?"

"In pediatric intensive care in Portland. He wasn't wearing a seatbelt."

Suddenly the condition of her car didn't seem so important. "Will he be okay?"

"It's too soon to say, although his prognosis isn't great. His family is with him. All we can do is pray." Mom took her hand and gave it a gentle squeeze. "Rest. I'll be right here if you need anything."

"What's the kid's name?"

"Zander Potts."

Nancy closed her eyes as the news sunk in.

"Do you know him?"

"We've met. I'm going to sleep. You don't need to stay."

"I understand, but I'll stay anyway."

"Mom, you have to work tomorrow. I'll feel horrible if something happens to you because you didn't get enough rest." Pain pulsed through her body. Hadn't they given her any meds? She didn't have the energy to ask.

Carter cleared his throat. "I have tomorrow off. I'll stay with her."

Nancy's pulse jumped again at his declaration. How would she sleep with him watching over her?

Mom nodded. "Very well. I'll go." She stood and kissed Nancy's forehead softly. "I'm glad you're okay."

Nancy resisted the urge to laugh. The pain wasn't worth it. "'Night."

Carter eased into the chair her mom had vacated. "My heart nearly stopped when I heard you'd been in an accident. I'll admit I broke the speed limit to get to you."

She grinned. "I don't believe you." Carter always gave her a hard time about her thirst for speed.

He chuckled as he grasped her hand. "Then that concussion is worse than I thought, because Lyle couldn't keep me away from you."

Her eyes shot open. "What're you talking about?"

"He happened by the accident right after it occurred and called me. You were wedged in there pretty good, and the fire department had to get you out. I'm shocked you don't have more injuries."

"I hurt everywhere. But I think my guardian angel was looking out for me."

"That fellow must work overtime," he teased playfully. He cleared his throat, his tone sobering. "Between you and my nephew, I think I've aged ten years since we've moved to Tipton. What were you doing anyway? I figured you'd be out walking and then at home preparing our dinner."

"I wanted to make a romantic meal. I needed a few things." Her dry throat caught, and she gagged. "Water," she rasped.

He grabbed the water bottle from beside her bed and held the straw to her lips. She sucked in a gulp then rested her head back against the pillow. "Thanks."

"You're welcome. I know this probably isn't the

time and you might not remember any of this later, but I realized something tonight."

Fatigue washed over her so she closed her eyes again and just listened.

"No matter how hard I try to protect you, I can't protect you from life. That's up to God, and I'm not Him."

She chuckled then gasped in pain.

"Shh." He grasped her hand gently in his. "I didn't mean to make you laugh, but I suppose that proves my point. Regardless of my best intentions, life happens, and I have no control over it."

She squeezed his hand. "I love you, Carter. Thank you for wanting to protect me." Her eyes shot open. Carter looked less surprised than she felt. Had those words really escaped her lips? Maybe it was the concussion talking. On second thought, she meant every word. Even though his desire to protect her frustrated her, deep down she appreciated that he cared enough to want to keep her safe.

"I love you too, sweetheart. I'm so thankful you're okay. I could have lost you today." He gently cupped her cheek. The loving gaze in his eyes made Nancy's sting. She'd been waiting her entire life for a man like him.

He pursed his lips. "You probably aren't up to talking shop, but as soon as you are, I'll brief you on Anna's situation. There's more there than you know, and I think it's time you were filled in."

She must be dreaming, but it was the best kind of dream. Carter loved her, and he was going to read her in—finally.

Chapter Fourteen

Anna hadn't been to Silver Creek Falls since she was a child. "We'll have to walk fast so we don't get stuck on the trail after dark." She still couldn't believe she had dropped everything to go on a hike with Titus. She wasn't an impulsive person, but with her life turned upside down, a spontaneous adventure was too good to pass up.

Titus parked and glanced her way. "We don't have to hike all the way around. We'll keep an eye on the light and figure it out as we go."

She climbed out of his pickup. "Works for me. Thanks for thinking of this. The chance of running into someone from Tipton way over here is slim. Plus, it's such a beautiful park."

"I agree. You ready?"

"Yes." Excitement coursed through her as they headed down the beginning of the trail. It was steeper than she remembered but being able to walk behind the roaring fall was worth it. The path soon narrowed, and they had to walk single file. Surprisingly, they were the only hikers in sight on the popular trail.

Erosion had ripped away the ground behind the falls that she'd walked on as a kid, and they had to duck to walk through the cave-like space. The roaring water made it difficult to hear anything, but she didn't mind one bit.

They passed under the fall and came out the

other side only slightly damp from the mist. Titus kept a steady pace but not so fast she couldn't keep up. All those evenings walking with Nancy were paying off. The trail widened, allowing her to stride beside him. "Is hiking a hobby of yours?"

"Yes," he said. "But I don't get to do it often enough. I haven't been out in nature since moving to Tipton."

"You must have missed it. It's so beautiful here. I can understand the allure." She looked up at the towering trees shading them.

"I didn't realize how much I missed it until now."

They hiked in companionable silence. Birds tweeted from their perch in the nearby trees. The sound of the water splashing into the pool that fed the creek below faded as they trekked along the man-made path. A squirrel darted across the path a few feet ahead of them and she caught her breath. They had plenty of squirrels in Tipton so her surprise was silly. The forest began to dim, and the sound of crickets rivaled the birds. "I think we'd better head back."

"We have been for a while now."

"Oh. Guess I wasn't paying attention." The lush beauty was quite a distraction. The steep path ahead made her groan. "I knew we'd have to climb back up, but it looks much steeper from this angle. That's so cruel."

"What?"

She pointed ahead. "An incline at the end of a hike."

"Would you like an elevator?"

She playfully punched his shoulder. "Be nice."

"I was." He grinned. "I'll race you to the top." He jogged ahead.

"Are you nuts!" She shouted after him. She might be in better shape than she was at the beginning of the school year, but no way could she run up that incline. She lengthened her stride and pumped her arms. She might not be able to run, but this technique proved to be a good one. Panting, she finally reached the top.

"Great job!" Titus raised his hand for a high-five.

She slapped it. "Thanks. That was fun. Maybe I should take up hiking." Although winded, she felt good. "Let's head into Silverton and grab dinner."

"I like how you think." He draped an arm casually across her shoulder.

Shock reverberated through her, not only that he would be so bold, but also that she didn't mind. "Where should we eat?"

"How about Creekside Grill? I've heard the food there is great, and they have outdoor seating that looks onto the water."

"That sounds perfect."

Anna gazed out at the creek behind Creekside Grill. The place lived up to its reputation for good food. The fish tacos were delicious. She wiped her fingers on her napkin. "That was the perfect ending to a not-so-perfect day. I think I'll actually sleep tonight. Thank you." If her head were on her pillow right now she had no doubt she'd be out.

"Thank *you*. I've had a great time too, and I'm glad to help get your mind off work."

"Let's not talk about work. I'm finally relaxed, and I'd like to end this evening on a positive note."

"Good thinking." He paid then they headed to his pickup for the hour-long drive back to Tipton.

Anna studied Titus's profile. "How come you're not married? You're a great guy. Good looking, smart, fun to be with…" She averted her gaze. Did she really want to know the answer?

He chuckled. "Thanks. I could ask the same of you."

"Nice deflection. I asked first."

He raised a brow.

"Fine. I'll go first. It's not a secret. I was once engaged, but my fiancé decided on the day of our wedding he didn't want to marry me."

"Ouch. I hope he at least had the courtesy to stop the wedding before it started."

"Well, it never started because no one could find him. All the guests were there, waiting. It was humiliating. I've guarded my heart since then. That was ten years ago." She'd gotten over being embarrassed by the story. The hurt had healed, but in its place, caution ruled. "Your turn."

"Ten years is a long time."

"It is." She wouldn't take the bait. "What about you?"

He took a breath and let it out. "Right. I've never told this to anyone."

Her senses heightened. "Thank you for trusting me. I won't abuse that trust."

"I know." Silence filled the cab for a few seconds.

"Eight years ago, shortly after I graduated from college, I proposed to my girlfriend."

"She said no?" What was wrong with that girl? Titus was a catch.

"Yes. I thought we were on the same page. But I was wrong. We ended up having a big fight the night I proposed. I was hurt and angry that she'd rather travel and see the world than marry me."

Anna shook her head. "You could have done that together."

"I agree, but that night I was too crushed to think clearly. After a couple of days, the same thought came to me. I tried calling her to tell her exactly that. I had it all worked out. I'd teach English abroad, and we could see the world together. Only she wouldn't take my calls." He took another breath and let it out slowly.

Anna's heart hurt for Titus. Talking about it even now seemed to bring him pain. She opened her mouth to tell him he didn't have to go on if it was too painful when he started talking again.

"I learned later that she had been hiding something from me. She had a stalker, and the reason she wanted to travel was to escape him. Only the stalker got to her before she could leave the country."

Anna gasped. "What happened?"

"I finally went over to her place and found the police there. Her family had requested a welfare check, and she was found dead inside her apartment—murdered. At first, I was their prime suspect. It was a nightmare."

"Wow. And I thought my story was bad. Did they

find her killer?"

"No. He's still out there somewhere." He glanced her way then returned his focus to the road. "Promise me, if you ever feel unsafe or that your life is in danger, you'll tell someone. Don't try to handle it on your own."

"That's what your girlfriend did?" Anna asked softly.

"Yes. Her sister suspected something was up with her but even she didn't know what was really going on. Once the police started digging, they discovered a box full of letters in her closet that the stalker had sent over the course of a month. I don't understand how I didn't know that something was up with her."

"She never hinted there was a problem?"

"Not once. I've gone over that month in my mind so many times. I don't understand why she never said anything. If only she'd told someone, she might still be alive. Don't make the same mistake, Anna."

She shivered and not from being cold. "I won't. I'm sorry that happened." There was so much about this man she didn't know. The hurt and pain from his past could have destroyed him, yet here he was trying to help her. He had a great job, and a lot of people thought highly of him.

"Thanks. I still struggle with it from time to time. To be honest, your situation kind of reminds me of Lizbeth."

Her body tensed. She didn't want to think whoever was trying to destroy her would actually kill her. "That was your girlfriend's name?"

"Yes."

A familiar sign grabbed her attention—they were

back in Tipton. The time had flown. As tired as she was she could probably talk with Titus for another hour, but they both had to get up early for work, and she needed her beauty sleep.

A few minutes later he pulled up in front of her house. "I'm sorry to end our evening on such a downer. It was never my intention to bring up Lizbeth."

"I'm glad you told me. It's the trials of life that make us who we are."

"Well said. Do you mind if I come by again soon?"

"I'd like that. But, Titus," she waited for him to face her, "I'm not Lizbeth, and our situations are different. I'm not being stalked, and I have people who are trying to figure this out." She reached over and took his hand. "Thank you for helping me to see that my situation isn't hopeless. I was feeling pretty low earlier and being with you tonight has really helped me see things differently."

The light from the streetlamp lit his face. His eyes softened. "I'm glad. It makes the pain of telling my story worth it."

Her heart melted. "You are a thoughtful and sweet man. Good night, Titus."

Titus waited until Anna was safely inside before heading for home. This day had been one surprise after another. He sure hadn't anticipated the late afternoon hike or dinner with Anna. Telling her about Lizbeth had been cathartic, and though it had been difficult, it was worth every heart-wrenching moment to share the burden he'd been hauling around for so many years.

Now what? The clock on the dashboard read nine-thirty. If he was smart he'd go home and get some shuteye, but he was too keyed up after spilling his deepest regret to Anna. He had never considered his story would make her feel better about her own situation. Keyed up or not, Rudy needed attention. He headed home.

For the first time since Lizbeth's death, he could picture himself with another woman, but the timing was horrible. Anna was in a mess up to her eyeballs. Good thing messes didn't scare him. Sure, they made him uncomfortable sometimes, but Anna needed all the support she could get right now, and he would be there for her no matter what—even if that meant messing up his own little world.

His cell phone rang. He answered with the Bluetooth. "Hello?"

"Titus. I need you." Panic filled Anna's voice.

"I'll be right there." He braked hard and did a U-turn.

Chapter Fifteen

Titus rapped his fist on Anna's front door. His heart still raced. *Lord please let her be okay.* His imagination had gone wild on the short drive back. He should have asked her what was wrong.

The door flung open. "Come in." Anna poked her head out and looked around for a moment. "Did you see anyone out there?"

"No. What's wrong? Is it Freddy?"

She shook her head and closed the door. "Thankfully, no. He's fine. But prepare yourself, it's gross." She took his hand and pulled him toward the back door grabbing a flashlight from beside the slider.

"Where's Freddy, Anna?" He'd heard her say her dog was fine, but why hadn't the little fellow greeted him?

"He's locked in my bedroom. When I got home I let him out to relieve himself. I followed him into the backyard and spotted a small lump in the shadows."

"A lump?" Dread shot through him. He took the flashlight from her hand. "What kind of lump? Should we call 911?"

"No. It's not an emergency, but I'll be filing a police report tomorrow." She stopped at the edge of the patio and pointed.

He clicked on the light, then shined it where Anna had indicated. What a vile joke. A dead rat lay in front of a makeshift cross that had the name

Freddy painted in red across it. He stepped closer. Unless he was mistaken, this rat appeared to have come from the anatomy lab: it had the identifying mark the school used for lab rats.

Had this sicko finally slipped and left them a much-needed clue to his identity? He turned and found Anna watching him with her arms wrapped around herself. "Do you have a plastic garbage bag?"

"I do, but I think we should leave it for the police. It's evidence. They might be able to get finger prints or something."

"Okay." Although he doubted there'd be any usable fingerprints since he was positive this came from the school's lab, and everyone who touched it would have been wearing gloves. He slid his thumb across the face of his phone and snapped several pictures, including a close-up of the cross. He'd send them to Anna later just in case anything happened to it overnight. "Let's get inside." He rested a hand on her back as they walked into her house. "I think you should stay with Nancy until this is all sorted out."

"That's a good idea. But if I stay with her it will probably come out that I'm being looked into by the administration. It's so embarrassing. I really don't want anyone to know, including Nancy."

"Sweetie, Nancy is your friend. Nothing you tell her is going to change that. Besides, in situations like this, word is bound to get out. There are no secrets in a town this size." He hadn't meant to call her sweetie, but Anna seemed so vulnerable and childlike it popped out. Hopefully, she hadn't noticed.

Her eyes pooled.

"Ah, Anna. I'm sorry. I thought you'd realize that."

She shrugged and looked like she'd lost her best friend. He pulled her into his arms. "Everything is going to be okay." He breathed in deeply of the light floral scent of her hair.

She rested her cheek and palm against his chest. "How can you say that? You have no way of knowing what something like this could do to my reputation if word got out—some people don't care about truth. Will I even have a job once this is over?" Her voice caught.

His heart broke for her as he rubbed her back. "I know you're innocent, and I believe Ms. Porter believes it too. I'm sure you'll still have your job when all is said and done." She relaxed in his arms. "I have a guest room. You and Freddy can stay there." His protective nature had clearly taken over good sense. The gossips would have a field day, but he didn't care.

"No. People will talk."

"I was thinking the same, but who cares. Your safety is more important. Let them talk. You care too much about what people think."

She pulled out of his embrace. He missed the feel of her in his arms. Was he falling for Anna? Or was this simply one friend comforting another? He didn't have time to evaluate his feelings right now. "Your safety is more important than what some busybody thinks."

She crossed her arms. "My reputation is very important to me. It's bad enough someone is trying to smear it but spending the night in your home would only make things worse."

He rubbed the back of his neck. "I don't know how far this kid will go, and I don't want you hurt. If you won't take me up on my offer, please go stay with Nancy."

"It's late. She's probably already in bed."

"Call her. I know she won't mind." He gave her his puppy-dog eyes look that had always worked when he was a kid.

A soft smile touched her lips. "Fine." She moved to the kitchen counter, dug her cell phone from her purse, and made the call. "Carter? I thought I was calling Nancy's phone." Her eyes widened. "Oh, no. What happened?" She pressed a button on the screen, setting it to speaker.

"Nancy was in a bad car accident earlier today. She's in the hospital, and I'm here with her."

Anna's stomach dropped. "Is she going to be okay?"

"Yes. But I should hang up. She's sleeping, and I don't want to disturb her. The nurses do that plenty already."

"Okay. If you need anything let me know."

"Thanks. She'll probably go home sometime tomorrow."

"I could stop in and check on her after school lets out."

"That'd be great." He sounded tired. "I'll be in touch. Thanks." He ended the call.

Titus frowned. "He hung up too fast. I was going to tell him about the rat in your backyard."

Anna set her phone on the kitchen counter. "He doesn't need to add that to his list of worries. His nephew must be spending the night alone."

"I imagine so. But he's old enough." What was he going to do about Anna? She couldn't stay here by herself with a maniac out there. The clock on the wall ticked away the seconds in the silent house.

"What are you thinking?" Anna stood facing him. She stuffed her hands into her jeans pockets.

"I'm trying to figure out how we are both going to get a restful night's sleep. I know for a fact if you stay here alone, I won't sleep a wink, and I suspect you won't either." Fear like he hadn't felt since discovering Lizbeth had been murdered caused acid to bubble in his gut. He hated this.

"I wouldn't be so sure." She yawned. "That hike and not sleeping last night are catching up to me. I'm sorry you're worried about me, but to be honest I don't think this kid wants to physically harm me, otherwise he would have done so already."

He understood why she thought that, but his experience had taught him people were full of surprises, and it was impossible to predict what this person might do next. Was the guy mentally unbalanced? Did he have anger issues? Was he a sick prankster? And what was his game? Until Titus had answers he wouldn't rest. "There has to be someone who you can stay with or invite over here for the night."

"It's almost ten o'clock, and I'm not going to intrude on anyone this late." She motioned for the door. "I appreciate all you've done and that you care so much, but I'm going to trust the Lord to watch out for me and Freddy. I'll call you first thing when I wake up tomorrow if that will make you feel better, but for now, it's time for you to go home." She wrapped a gentle hand around his arm and nudged him toward the door.

He didn't want to leave but knew better than to force the issue. He moved forward with her urging. "Okay. You win. I'll go. But if you don't call me by six-thirty, expect a knock on your door by seven."

She chuckled. "You planning to skip school?" She removed her hand from his arm as she stopped beside the front door. "I'll be in my car on my way to work at that time."

He raised his chin. "It's going to be a long night."

Her eyes sparkled. What could she possibly be so happy about? She stood up on tiptoe and placed a kiss on his cheek. "You're one of a kind, Titus. I'll call you. And stop worrying. I'm not Lizbeth."

He hadn't expected her to kiss him—even if it was only a peck on his cheek. He probably had a dopey look on his face because his insides had turned to mush.

"Now go." She pulled open the door and lightly pushed him out.

The following morning, Anna woke to the sound of her doorbell. She kicked off the covers and stretched. Several firm raps caused her to reach for her robe. Who would be at her door so early? She glanced at the bedside clock and gasped. Seven o'clock. She'd overslept.

"Titus!" He must be freaking out. She slid her robe over her T-shirt and sweatpants as she raced to the door.

Freddy barked repeatedly as he jetted ahead of

her and slid to a stop. He reared up on his back legs with every bark. Anna yanked open the door. "Titus, I'm so sorry. I must have forgotten to set my alarm." He didn't look like he'd slept at all last night. She gasped. "Are you okay?"

His face relaxed. He let out his breath in a puff and sagged against the door jam. "You took ten years off my life this morning when you didn't call like you'd promised. I even tried texting and calling you but got no response."

"I'm really sorry, but I overslept and didn't hear my phone. Come in. Will you make me coffee while I get ready? I have a couple to-go mugs in the cupboard. Make yourself one too. You look like you could use it." She raced toward the hallway.

"Thanks," he said drily. He stepped inside and headed to the kitchen. Hopefully the coffee brewed fast. Although he could get away with being a few minutes late to work, she couldn't—not with a roomful of students waiting.

Ten minutes later she rushed into the kitchen, threw together a peanut butter and jelly sandwich, then tossed it along with an apple into a brown paper bag. "The coffee ready?"

"Yes, but I didn't know how you like it." He slid the travel thermos toward her. "I found half and half in the fridge, but figured you'd want to add it yourself."

She tipped a generous splash into the mug then twisted on the lid. "We have to go. Now!" She grabbed her purse, lunch, and coffee and ran toward the door.

He was right behind her. "Wait! What about Freddy?"

"I'm not going to get to class on time if I wait for him to do his thing outside."

"Tell you what. Since I don't have any classes to rush off to, I'll stay, feed him, let him into the yard then bring him inside when he's done. I'll lock up. You can get your keys from me later."

"Perfect." She slid a key off her ring and tossed it to him. "I owe you."

"And I'll collect."

Anna's day still felt like a whirlwind, but she had begun to catch her breath around midmorning. She'd made it to her classroom as the bell rang. Someone, probably Luke, had unlocked the door already and allowed her students to enter. The teachers often did that for one another when one of them was running late.

The morning passed uneventfully. When the lunch bell rang, her class cleared rapidly. She locked the door and went in search of Titus. She poked her head into the teachers' lounge. Luke stood at the microwave but didn't notice her. Titus wasn't there. She closed the door softly and headed for his office.

She peered through the window and rapped on it. He looked up from his computer and motioned her inside.

"Hi. How'd it go with Freddy?"

"He took his merry ole time and kept running over to sniff and growl at the rat, but otherwise all went well. I'm glad I took those pictures though, because as I thought might happen, something got to the rat."

She winced. "Gross. I really appreciate all you've done for me."

"I'm glad I could be there." He pulled her house key from his pocket and placed it on his desk.

"Thanks." She added it back to the ring.

"Where's your lunch?"

"I ate it about an hour ago. I'm not used to skipping breakfast."

He nodded then stood. "We could do a burger run to BLB."

"Listen to you. You sound like a native Tiptonite speaking in code." She laughed. "As good as that sounds, I doubt Best Little Burger can make it fast enough."

"They can if I order ahead." He pulled out his phone. "What do you want?" He waggled his brows.

Her stomach did a little flip as she giggled. She needed to get a grip. She cleared her throat. "A cheeseburger, no onion or pickles."

He placed their orders then stood. "You ready?"

"Yep." They raced like a couple of teenagers through the hall toward the exit doors. "I can't believe we're doing this." She panted as she jogged beside him.

"What? Cutting out for lunch?"

"Yes."

Chapter Sixteen

NANCY RESTED, SITTING PROPPED UP ON her living room sofa. Carter had brought her home and still hovered nearby in the kitchen. "You really don't need to stay with me. I know you should return to work. Plus, I'm sure Gavin would like to see his uncle sometime today."

He walked back into the living room holding two mugs. "Tea for you, and coffee for me." He handed her the cup. "As for my nephew, I've kept in touch with him via text. He had dinner at Maddie's last night. I told Luke what was going on, and he offered their guest room to Gavin. He's fine. But he did tell me that something is going on with Anna. Any idea what?" He sipped from his mug.

"Hmm. I have no idea. I saw her drive off with Titus yesterday late in the afternoon. Maybe that's what he's talking about."

"I don't think so." He sat in an easy chair facing her. "Anna called last night and asked for you. I should've pressed her."

Nancy's need-to-know gene kicked in. Something was definitely up with her friend. "Anna never calls, only texts. Have there been any further developments regarding her case? Maybe something else happened."

"Unfortunately, you're probably right."

"You mentioned that you had something to tell me. I feel like we are on the cusp of something big, but I'm missing a key component to the puzzle." If only her head would stop hurting, she might be able to fit the pieces together and figure out who was behind Anna's trouble, and then the school could deal with him.

A rap sounded on the front door. Nancy leaned forward to get it.

"Oh, no you don't. The doctor said you needed to rest today. I'll answer the door."

"Thanks." Relief washed over her. If she were honest, rest was exactly what her body craved, but this thing with Anna wouldn't leave her alone. She was missing something important.

A moment later Carter returned with Anna.

Nancy took in the woman's appearance—dark wash jeans, with a red blazer over a white blouse. "You went shopping without me." Disappointment hit her but quickly faded as she realized how sharp her friend looked. She was a far cry from the frumpily dressed woman she used to know. "You look great. Those clothes fit you perfectly."

"Thanks." She posed with a hand at her waist and one shoulder forward.

Nancy chuckled and immediately regretted it. "Oww. Don't make me laugh."

Anna sobered. "Sorry. The consignment shop over on Front Street had it. A friend of mine works there. I asked her to keep an eye out for stuff she thought I might like. When she called I rushed over. I couldn't wait for you, or it might have been gone." Anna sat in the easy chair that Carter had been in. "How are you feeling?"

Carter eased onto the arm of the couch. Nancy

scooted her legs up, leaving room for Carter to join her. "I'll share." She turned her attention to Anna. "All things considered, I'm feeling okay." Which was relative in this case. Her head still ached, and her entire body hurt.

"I'm thankful you weren't seriously injured." Anna looked toward Carter. "I'm glad you're here. I planned to call the police today but never got around to it. I didn't want to bother you with this, but since you're here..."

"What's up?"

Anna took a breath and let it out slowly. "Sometime yesterday, I'm guessing last night, someone left the carcass of a lab rat in my backyard. Titus believes it was stolen from the high school."

"Are you sure it wasn't just a dead rat? That wouldn't be too hard to imagine."

"Yes." She pulled out her phone. "Titus took a few pictures. A cat or something got to it last night, but these tell it all."

Carter reached for the device, swiped through the pictures, and frowned. "Make sure you file a police report. When we catch this guy, it'll be used to build our case against him. Is any of it still there?"

She nodded. "Not much, but the cross is fully intact. Titus thought there might be fingerprints."

"It's possible. But the prints would need to be in the system for it to matter. My gut tells me we won't find a match."

Anna nodded. "I really need help and fast. This person is trying to destroy me. I can't say for certain that it's the same person, but someone filed a complaint accusing me of helping students cheat on tests."

"That's terrible." Nancy looked at Carter. Hadn't he said he had a lead—maybe not his exact words, but it was implied. Nancy hurt for her friend and wanted more than anything to solve this mystery. Anna loved teaching. Whoever was out to make her miserable was doing a very good job. "Carter, you said you had something to tell me regarding Anna's situation?"

He shook his head.

Oops. It looked like he didn't want to talk about it in front of Anna, but this involved her, so it only seemed fair to include her friend. "You can trust Anna."

He sighed. "I suppose it wouldn't be breaking any rules. Gavin overheard a few boys talking in the locker room. One was bragging about getting back at you."

Shock and pain registered on Anna's face. "Seriously? Who was it?"

"That's the problem. Gavin was on the other side of the lockers, and when he walked around them to see who the boys were, they were gone. However, I was able to procure a list of the boys in PE for that period. Lucky for us, there are only twenty."

"Twenty is a lot." Anna's shoulders slumped. "I wish I knew who I'd upset and how. Clearly whatever it was made a huge impact on this kid's life. You'd think I'd know."

"Yeah." Nancy frowned. "I'm with Anna. Whatever happened sounds big—or at least this kid perceives it as life changing. Think hard, Anna. There has to be something. Maybe a kid came to you for advice and things didn't turn out like he expected, or maybe you gave someone a bad grade which caused him to be on academic probation and not able to play in sports. Or it could be as simple as you gave a high achieving student a B—a grade like that could impact college financial aid if they were on a GPA bubble."

"I've done nothing but think. I hadn't considered a grade could push a person over the edge, but I can see how it might."

"We need a list of all your students who don't have an A in your class so we can cross reference them with the names from the PE class and the classes that were dissecting rats that day."

"Good idea," Carter said. "Can you get that for me, Anna?"

"I think so. The list will be a lot longer than those twenty boys. I have a lot of students."

"We only need the names of the males and then only the ones in the PE class. The names of students in the science lab class would be helpful too, if you can get it. The kid might not be in that class though, so it could be a long shot. It wouldn't be too difficult for someone to break into the lab and steal one of the carcasses."

"Okay. I'll work on that right now. The records are all online—I can access my students' records with no problem." She pulled out her phone again. "Do you have paper, Nancy?"

"There's a notepad on the kitchen counter."

"I'll get it." Carter stood.

"Are you able to move around okay?" Anna asked softly.

"Yes, but slowly."

"Good. Would you mind having a couple of roomies until they find this kid? Titus was pretty upset last night and insisted I not stay alone."

"Really? Is there something going on between the two of you? I saw you getting into his pickup yesterday."

Carter handed Anna the pad and a pen, then sat.

"He's a friend."

"Only a friend?" Nancy would love to see Anna find true love, but she didn't see a sparkle in the woman's eyes like she'd expected. Maybe all that was going on made it difficult to relax enough to make a love connection. Or maybe there was someone else. No, Anna hadn't talked about any other man. It had to be the stress of being investigated.

"For now." A gentle smile tipped her lips.

Ah, now there was the look Nancy expected to see. If she didn't hurt all over she'd do a little dance.

Carter cleared his throat. "Luke Harms has been calling me daily to check the progress of our investigation into who is harassing Anna."

Anna's eyes widened. "Really? I didn't know that."

"He seems incredibly concerned about you."

"He's the head of the English department. I imagine he's anxious about the situation and how it's affecting my work and students."

"Maybe, but it felt like more than that to me. I don't know him well, so I could be wrong." Carter stood. "If you feel you can manage on your own, Nancy, I should head out."

"I'll be fine. Plus, Anna and Freddy will be bunking here for the time being."

"Good." He planted a kiss on Nancy's lips. "I'll call

later," he said, then left.

Nancy sighed.

Anna giggled. "True love."

"You could be right, my friend." She motioned toward the pad of paper that Anna had yet to write a single name on. "How's the list coming?"

"I got distracted." She turned her attention to her phone and began jotting down names. "This was such a great idea. I'm sure we'll figure out who's behind this now. After all, how many boys could I have in my English classes with a grade below an A and who are also in that PE class?" She glanced at Nancy then back at her phone. "What made you go into Library Science rather than law enforcement? You seem to have a knack for following clues."

"I enjoy a good mystery, but actual crime fighting is not my thing. I'll leave that to the professionals. Speaking of a good mystery, I wish I had some books at home. I've read everything I have here. I'd planned to check out a couple of new ones today. Since I'm supposed to take it easy I have no idea how I will entertain myself. Then again, the doctor warned me, reading might be painful."

"I'm sorry. I know how you enjoy a good book. But I have a solution for your boredom." Anna tapped the pad of paper. "We'll go through each and every name. Maybe we could show our final list of suspects to Gavin. Perhaps seeing the name will trigger a memory of the boy's voice."

"It's a good idea, but Carter is firm about leaving Gavin out of this. I want to respect his wishes."

"Okay. I'll do a little reconnaissance on my own then."

Nancy grinned. "Listen to you. You sound like me."

"I do, don't I?" Anna tapped the pad with the top of the pen. "Since you're out of commission awhile, it's up to me to be your eyes and ears."

Nancy studied her friend who wasn't exactly a thrill seeker. What had brought out this new side to Anna? "You sure about that? This kid could be dangerous. He really seems out of balance."

"I'm sure, but I hope you're wrong about him. I'd like to believe he's simply a creative person bent on making my life difficult."

"You really surprise me, Anna. I know you're strong, but you have moxie."

Anna chuckled. "Speaking of moxie, I should go get Freddy. Do you think he'd be safe playing in your backyard?"

"I don't see why not, unless this kid is following you to keep an eye on you."

Anna's gaze slammed into Nancy's. "Do you think he's stalking me?"

"Not likely. Just be careful." She didn't want her friend to worry needlessly, but she was also a realist and wanted her to be careful.

Fear filled Anna's eyes.

Nancy sighed. "It was a dumb thing to say. Sorry. I didn't mean to worry you any more than you are already."

"It's fine. I should be vigilant. But, going on the assumption that this is a top student, I imagine his school work is more important than stalking me or Freddy."

"See. You proved my point—it was a dumb thing to say."

Anna stood. "Will you be okay here by yourself for a bit? It might take me a while to pack up everything we'll need for a few days."

"Take your time." Nancy waited until she heard the click of the front door then closed her eyes. *Lord, I appreciate You providing me with help via Anna. Please help us to find this kid who's harassing her, and please heal my body quickly. Thanks.*

Anna had left the notepad next to the list of students in the PE class. Nancy reached for the lists and the pen then started to cross-reference the lists. Sometime later a light knock sounded on her front door. "Come in."

The front door opened, and a moment later Freddy darted into the room and trotted over to greet her. "Hi, boy." She scratched his white head. She looked up as Anna dropped a pile of stuff onto the floor.

"What's all of that?"

"The necessities. Dog food, Freddy's bowl, his bed, toys…"

"I get the picture. Make yourselves at home. Once you're settled, I want to show you the names I've come up with so far." It wasn't a big list, but maybe one of the names would stand out to her.

"Already? I haven't finished going through all my students."

"We can add to the list."

After a while they had five names. Anna grinned. "I didn't think we could narrow it down to such a small list. And it's actually smaller than this since you included Gavin's name." She waved the sheet of paper in the air. "Surely the authorities will be able to find this kid now."

"Or *we* could." Nancy raised her brows. "How hard could it be to investigate four boys?"

Anna frowned. "In your condition? I don't think so. Besides, I think this kind of thing is best left to the police."

"Party pooper." Nancy knew her friend was right, but she refused to give up. That would be admitting defeat—unacceptable. But before she did anything else she needed to rest her peepers. The doctor's warning rang true—reading did make her head hurt.

Anna pulled books from her tote bag. "I happened to have a couple books at my place I thought you might enjoy." She handed them to Nancy.

"Would you believe I've already read them?"

"Of course you have." Anna rolled her eyes.

"Tell you what. Give me fifteen minutes to take a power nap then we'll run this list over to Luke."

"Why not text it to him?"

Nancy blew out a breath. "Fine." One way or another, she'd solve this mystery—even if that meant inserting herself into the thick of it at the sheriff's department.

Chapter Seventeen

A WEEK AFTER THE INVESTIGATION INTO the accusation against Anna, Luke pushed back from his desk at school and stood. He'd presented his findings to his boss, and Anna's name would be cleared—at least that's what he hoped. He'd found nothing that gave him concern, including her students' grades which were consistent with the school average department-wide. If Anna was giving out test answers, then every teacher in the school was. There simply was no evidence to support the claim.

He couldn't wait to see Anna and tell her. He found Ms. Porter in her office. "I emailed you my report regarding Anna Plum."

She looked up from whatever she'd been working on, rested her elbows on her desk, and laced her fingers. "Come in and close the door."

Nervousness struck him. He did as she'd asked then sat. "What's up?"

"I had an interesting phone call a short time ago."

"About...?" Something in the tone of her voice set him on edge.

"Sheriff Daley said there is an open investigation regarding a rat cadaver that was stolen from the school lab and placed in Anna's backyard a week ago. This is the first I've heard of it. What do you know?"

"Nothing. I've avoided her like you instructed." He would have seen her once if she had been home, but that didn't count.

"Someone here must've filed a police report for them to know the rat came from the school."

"I'm at a loss. I know nothing about this. Why not call Anna and ask her?"

"Good idea. But I have my hands full. Since you've finished with your part of the investigation, you're free to talk to her about this other matter."

He'd love an excuse to talk with her again. "I'd be happy to deliver the good news."

"Good news?"

What was going on with Ms. Porter? She was acting strange. "Yes. Her name has been cleared of helping students cheat." Hadn't that been the point of asking him to look into her students' records—to clear her name.

She shook her head. "You're mistaken. The investigation is not complete. Your findings still need to be sorted through. I'll be the one to notify Anna when this is over. Thanks for putting in extra hours to get this done. I'm sure she'll appreciate it."

Irritation shot through him. "You mean to tell me, after all I did, you're not satisfied?"

She narrowed her eyes. "I saw your report as soon as it hit my inbox, but I must do due diligence as well. I believe Anna is innocent, but if there's even a hint of truth to the complaint..."

Unbelievable. He stood. "I see. What do I tell Anna?"

"The truth, and while you're at it, find out about that rat. This should've been reported to me immediately. I was made to look like a fool. When I retire at the end of this school year, I don't want this marring my reputation."

Unwilling to trust himself to speak respectfully to his boss, he only said goodbye and left. Ms. Porter seemed to be on the warpath, and he didn't want to get caught in the middle. He couldn't help Anna if he got booted. The best thing he could do was play nice. But he wasn't happy about it. Not one bit.

Since Gavin was walking Maddie home, he was on his own today. A sudden thought hit him, and a slow smile spread across his face.

Thirty minutes later he parked in front of Anna's house. The glass vase filled with spring flowers sitting on the passenger seat gave him pause—maybe flowers were a bit much. His wife had loved flowers, and he'd never needed a special occasion to give them to her, but Anna wasn't his wife. In fact, she was nothing like her. They were opposites in every way. JC had been petite and the life of the party, and Anna was of average build and quiet and didn't laugh much—at least around him. He'd seen her laughing with others though, so he might be wrong about her in that regard.

Speaking of Anna. She waved as she walked beside Nancy toward her house. Her cheeks had a healthy glow. She wore running pants with a purple shirt that hung down to the middle of her thighs and a black hoodie. He'd never seen her look so relaxed. His pulse amped.

"Here goes nothing." He took a calming breath and stepped out with the vase of flowers. He walked around the front of his car and stood on the sidewalk.

Anna said something to Nancy then the woman went to her own house. "Hi, Luke. What's going on?

I'm surprised to see you here." She met him on the curb beside his car.

"I'm glad I caught you. I stopped by last week and missed you."

Her brow wrinkled. "Really? When?"

"Around four, the day after I told you about the accusation against you."

"Oh." Confusion covered her face then awareness. "I must've been in the bathroom when you stopped by. I'd been cleaning house. I'm sorry I missed you."

"It was fine." He'd gone out of his way to avoid her at work, since he was looking into her students' records, but no way would he reveal that to her. They'd be right back where they used to be, and he rather liked their new friendship. He held the flowers out to her. "These are for you."

"Thank you. They're beautiful, but why did you get me flowers?"

"I thought you could use something to brighten your day."

She frowned. "You've come with bad news?"

"No. Not exactly. Is there a place we can talk?" He'd hoped the flowers would ease the jolt of hearing what he had to tell her, but clearly he didn't know Anna all that well.

"Sure. We can sit in the backyard. Freddy will enjoy running around, even if he is worn out from the walk. We haven't been home ever since..." She pressed her lips together.

"Ever since what?"

She sighed. "Let's get Freddy in, and I'll tell you."

For the first time he noticed the little white dog standing beside her. "He's quiet today."

"His walks mellow him, plus he's been getting a lot of extra attention from Nancy. We've been staying at her place." She turned and strolled toward the house.

He followed, more than a little curious about why she was staying with her neighbor. "Is there a problem with your house?"

A puzzled look crossed her face then cleared. "Oh. I see why you'd think that. But no, there's nothing wrong with my house." She unlocked the door then they walked through the stuffy house to the backyard. "Would you like something to drink?"

"No thanks but feel free if you need something."

She shook her head. "I'll get something in a bit." She pulled the slider open and let Freddy off his leash.

"This sure is a nice set up." The covered patio with two chairs faced a grassy yard with flowerbeds along the perimeter and some kind of a maple tree off to one side. He hadn't paid much attention the last time he'd stopped by.

"Thanks." She sat and motioned toward the other chair.

"Why are you staying with your neighbor?"

"You first. What news do you have? As lovely as the flowers are, why do I need them to brighten my day?" Her folded hands revealed white knuckles. Clearly, she felt uneasy.

"I was tasked with looking into your students' records."

Her lips parted, and she inhaled sharply. "I suppose that shouldn't surprise me, but it does."

"It surprised me too. I never expected to be thrust into the middle of this. Anyway, I've completed my investigation, and I'm happy to say that I found nothing to incriminate you." His thoughts drifted to the note that had been taped to his door. It had told him to look into Riley Bates, but he'd found nothing unusual. Had he missed something their boss would find? He'd tossed the note, but he couldn't help but wonder if that had been a mistake. What if there had been a way to trace it back to whomever was out to get Anna?

She smiled. The white knuckled grip on her fingers eased. "You had me worried. So my name is cleared. That's great news!" She jumped up.

"No." He raised his voice above hers.

Her face blanked. "What?"

"Please sit, Anna." He waited for her to sink back down. "Ms. Porter will be following up on my investigation. It's not over yet."

Her mouth opened slightly. "But you said there's no evidence against me."

"I know, and I'm as baffled as you. I wish I had more info, but I don't know why she wants to keep looking into the situation. Maybe she's just being thorough."

Anna's eyes glazed. He wanted to tell her everything would be okay, but he honestly didn't know if it would. Their boss's attitude concerned him. Was it that she'd been embarrassed for not knowing about the missing cadaver, or was there more?

He waited until Anna's eyes cleared, and she looked his direction. "There's something else."

She sighed. "What now?"

"Sheriff Daley questioned Ms. Porter about a cadaver that apparently came from the school's lab."

She shrugged her shoulders. "And?"

"And Ms. Porter was unhappy about it not being

reported to her. I think she was embarrassed."

Anna crossed her arms. "I didn't realize I needed to let her know. Seems to me the anatomy teacher should've done that since it was taken from her class."

"I agree."

"I'm surprised that Titus didn't say something since he's the one who ended up telling the police it came from the school."

"Titus knew?" Disappointment filled him. He'd noticed the man had spent time with Anna and had also heard through the grapevine they'd been spotted together on more than one occasion, but he hadn't thought much of it until now.

"Yes. He and I, uh… went out last week. When I returned, I let Freddy out here and discovered the rodent. I called Titus, and he came over. He said the anatomy lab had been dissecting the rat in class that same day. I assumed the teacher would deal with reporting it to Ms. Porter."

So the rumors were true. Disappointment shot through him. Why had he allowed his attraction to Anna to grow? He should have known she'd never be interested in him. "I'd have expected the same. I should head home. Maddie will wonder where I am."

She stood. "I'll walk you to the door. Do you have any idea how much longer the investigation will take?"

"I'm afraid not." He followed her inside. "Ms. Porter was still in her office when I left. You could try calling her or wait until school tomorrow."

She stopped beside her front door. "Ms. Porter has been giving me weird looks at school this past week. She's making me nervous."

"I understand. I'd feel the same way. Hang in there, Anna. This will all be over soon, and then we can resume annoying one another."

She chuckled. "I knew you annoyed *me*, but I had no idea it went both ways."

He winked and left, pleased he'd gotten her to smile. Too bad though about Titus. At least he found out sooner than later. But he couldn't help the disappointment.

Maybe things wouldn't work out between Titus and Anna, and then he could swoop in.

Nancy took advantage of having her home to herself while Anna visited with Luke at her place. She pulled the slip of paper from her nightstand drawer with the names of the suspects. "Riley Bates, Gavin Malone, James Jensen, Robert Prescott, Jordan Black." The police had questioned each of the boys then dismissed all of them as suspects—Nancy didn't accept their conclusion. One of them had to be their guy.

To Nancy's way of thinking only three of them were clear: Gavin, Riley, and Robert. That only left James and Jordan. She'd met both boys since they were regular library patrons. They were underclassmen and wouldn't have been eligible to enter the writing contest. Had the clues led them down the wrong trail?

"I'm back." The front door whooshed closed.

"Okay." Nancy slid the slip of paper back into the drawer then padded out to the living room. A vase filled with spring flowers sat on the kitchen table.

"Those are pretty."

"Yes. Luke brought them over." Anna stood beside the table with Freddy lying at her feet.

Nancy's brows rose. "That doesn't sound like the man you once described as a curmudgeon."

Anna shrugged. "People change. Luke's actually been great through all of this." Her face pinked.

Nancy grinned. "What aren't you saying?" She snuggled into the corner of the couch.

Anna shifted from one foot to the other. "I think I might have led Luke on, and that's why he brought me flowers." She sighed and plopped into the nearest chair.

"What did you do?"

Anna buried her face in her hands. "It's so embarrassing now that I realize it." She took a breath and let it out fast. "Luke delivered the news about the complaint against me. I was super upset and feeling out of sorts. He was being so nice and when he asked if I needed anything, I asked for a hug."

Nancy gasped then slapped a hand to her mouth. "Sorry, go on."

Anna shook her head. "That's it. But it's enough. He didn't hesitate to comfort me, but I realized too late that I'd made him uncomfortable." A pained look crossed her face. "What do I do now?"

"You're asking me? You are far more experienced than I am when it comes to men."

Anna chuckled. "Now that you're dating Carter, I guess I forgot your lack of experience. To be honest, I'm not all that experienced either. Luke intrigues me, and he's surprisingly sweet with a romantic side, but Titus is so..."

"Gorgeous?"

Anna chuckled. "I have to admit, it's flattering to have a man like him pay attention to me."

Concern nibbled at the back of Nancy's mind. "But?"

"But I'm not sure he's the one."

"I see. How will you know who *the one* is?"

Anna shrugged. "My heart will tell me, I guess."

"Hmm." Her heart told her Carter was the one, but what if her heart was wrong? She'd been pondering this dilemma for a while now and was no closer to knowing the answer. She shook away the thought to focus on her friend. "Besides the flowers, did Luke want anything?"

Anna sighed and sank into the nearest chair. "He had news, but it was mixed."

Nancy sat. "Uh-oh."

"Uh-oh is right. It seems my boss thinks there's some truth to the complaint."

"Why? Did Luke tell you that?"

She shook her head. "Not in so many words. He said he'd finished his investigation and couldn't find anything to substantiate the claim that I've been helping students cheat, but when he reported his findings to our boss she wasn't satisfied. She's following up on his investigation."

"What's that supposed to mean?" Nancy tensed. She'd hoped at least one thing would go right for her friend. It was bad enough someone was harassing her, she didn't need this ridiculous claim to drag on.

"It means my name hasn't been cleared yet."

Chapter Eighteen

Titus eased up beside Anna as she walked briskly through the hallway during lunch. "How's it going?"

She glanced his way with a furrowed brow. "Okay."

"Really? You don't look okay. Has something else happened?"

"Not really. I'm just uptight today. Ms. Porter chewed me out for not telling her about finding the rat from the anatomy class in my yard. When I explained what has been going on, she chewed me out all over again for not keeping her up-to-date." She stopped and faced him. "Am I crazy? I don't see how any of this is her business."

Titus grimaced. "Knowing the kind of person she is, I should have seen this coming. I'm sorry for not saying something."

Anna's face softened. "There's no need to apologize. I suppose I should have known as well. I guess I expected her to know since we involved IT from the start. I figured someone was reporting to her. I shouldn't have assumed."

Anna didn't need their boss coming down on her right now. She had enough to deal with. Thankfully, Ms. Porter's days were numbered at Tipton High. "Are you going to be okay?" He rested a hand on her shoulder.

She stiffened. "Yes. I'm just venting."

"Okay. If you ever need to talk, you know where to find me. Or call me anytime."

"I appreciate that." The five-minute warning bell rang. "I need to get to class."

He waved as she hustled down the hall and into the sea of students making their way to classrooms. He went to his office and closed the door. Anna's response to his touch troubled him. Hadn't they been on the path to more than friendship? Had something changed since they'd last been together? *Lord did I misunderstand? I could sure use Your wisdom.*

Maybe it was for the best since he'd been asked to consider becoming the next principal at Tipton High School. Having a relationship with a teacher while he was the principal was a bad idea, which is why he hadn't given his answer yet. He really liked Anna and had thought there might be something there, but maybe it had more to do with her crisis than true feelings.

He needed to give his answer about the position soon. Troubled, he turned his attention to his computer. He had work to do and trying to figure out Anna seemed to be an exercise in futility. He'd never been able to figure out a woman's mind. Apparently, he still couldn't.

After school Anna gazed out her classroom window. Her life, both professionally and personally was messy, and she didn't like it—not one bit. She despised being chewed out by her boss. After all, she was the victim. Shouldn't Ms. Porter be there to support her, not make her feel bad for her lack of communication?

The authorities as well as Nancy were no closer to figuring out who was making her life difficult, and her feelings for Titus were all over the place. He was a good man with a big heart, but if she were honest, she was more flattered by his attention than anything romantic. She enjoyed his company and spending time with him, but she felt the same way about Luke—who would have thought that could ever happen? Not her. Other than the flowers he'd brought by—which she assumed was to ease the blow of his news—Luke didn't seem interested in her, at least that she could see. But he was a difficult man to figure out. Had she completely missed her chance at love? More than that though, was she even capable of loving again?

"Miss Plum?"

Anna shook away her thoughts and turned toward the door where one of her former students stood. "Hi, Lauren. This is a surprise. Come in."

Lauren walked into the room, leaving the door open. She kept her voice low. "Do you remember the time we talked about my...um, boyfriend?"

Anna nodded as she moved to the chair behind her desk and motioned for Lauren to take a seat at the desk nearest hers.

An anxious look covered Lauren's face. Her fingers were laced tightly on the desktop. "The thing is, he wants to get back together. I told him no, but he won't leave me alone."

Anna's shoulders tensed. "Do you feel threatened

or in danger?"

"No. But he's being a pain, and I don't know what to do. If he cares so much about me, maybe I should give him a chance."

"Is he serving the Lord now?"

Lauren shrugged. "I don't think so. But he said he'd go to church with me."

Evangelist dating, as her mom had called it was not a good idea, but how did she communicate this to Lauren? "My mom used to tell me that I couldn't date a guy unless he attended our church."

"Your mom was strict." Lauren made a face as if she'd tasted something gross.

"Perhaps, but I appreciated that she cared enough to help me set boundaries. I'm not saying going to church makes a person a Christian, only that it was one of the rules of my house. I realized, and so did my mom, that church was a starting-point criteria." She chuckled. "There was this guy that I had a huge crush on in high school. I told my mom about him, and she asked if he went to our church—he didn't. That's when I learned about the rule. I was so angry with my mom. I eventually saw the wisdom of it, but at the time, I was not happy." She shook her head. "The worst part was he didn't know I existed. I never had a chance with him so getting angry with my mom was irrational and a waste of energy."

"Sometimes our feelings are irrational."

Anna's eyes widened. "You're wise beyond your years. What do *you* think you should do?"

"I don't know."

"Have you talked with your mom or any other trusted adults?"

She shook her head. "No. My mom doesn't like him, and I figured since you know him and me and since you and I go to the same church, you'd be the best person to talk to."

Anna sighed. In many ways Lauren reminded her of herself. She knew the answer, but she didn't like it, so she sought out advice from others. "Why did you break up to begin with?"

"Because he was pressing me to do something I didn't want to do."

"Right. And has that changed?"

"I don't know. Probably not."

Advising a student about boys fell outside her job description, and she'd never felt so underqualified to answer a question. "I'm not comfortable telling you what to do, but praying has always helped me."

Lauren frowned and nodded. "Okay. Good idea. But what if I don't like the answer?"

"Then you'll have a decision to make. Obey or not. I suggest obedience. It's a losing battle to fight the Lord. Believe me, I know this from experience."

Lauren nodded and stood. "Thanks, Miss Plum. What you said makes a lot of sense. I think the only reason I'm considering getting back with him is because I like his attention, and I liked having a boyfriend."

Anna raised a brow. "Do you think those are valid reasons?"

"They're valid but not good."

Anna breathed a little easier. "Promise me something. If he ever makes you feel afraid, like he might hurt you, I want you to get help. Tell someone, go to the police. Do whatever you need to do."

"I will, but he's not like that. He's a good guy. He just doesn't like the word no."

Anna stood and walked with the girl to the door. "At least you'll be off at college next year and won't need to worry about him."

"True. And there will be lots of college guys." She smiled and slipped from the room.

Anna returned to her desk. She needed to follow her own advice and pray. *Lord, please take care of Lauren. I'm concerned for her. I know she doesn't feel threatened by her old boyfriend, but the situation makes me feel uneasy.*

I could use some guidance regarding my own love life—not that I really have one. But You know Luke and Titus, and I'm kind of interested in both of them, at least I think I might be. Titus is so good looking and such a nice guy, but there's not a spark with him when we're together. Well, there was a spark at first, but not now. Does that mean there's no hope for us?

What about Luke, Lord? He's changed so much. I'm drawn to him but for completely different reasons. Please help me to know what to do—if anything. And please help me to accept Your answer. Thanks. Amen.

The Lord had never failed her, even when she didn't like the answer. Through the years she'd realized that His way was always the best way. It probably would seem strange to people if they knew she talked to the Lord about men, but He knew her the best. So who better to guide her?

"Knock. Knock." Luke walked into her classroom and ambled up to her desk. "I've been meaning to ask about the writing contest. I noticed the finalists were posted. When is the deadline for their revisions?"

"Midnight tonight."

"Excellent. Please send them as soon as you have them. I'm really looking forward to judging them. To be honest I'm surprised, but I missed it this year."

Her eyes widened. "You're kidding."

"Turns out I enjoy being a judge." He chuckled. "Who knew? As I'm sure you figured out, running it and judging are two different things."

A stiff breeze could have blown her over she was so surprised. "Okay. I'll do that. I have all but one."

He eased onto the top of one of the student desks. "How are things going?" He lowered his voice. "Have there been any developments with anything?"

She shook her head. "No. It's been quiet—too quiet actually. I wonder if the kid has grown bored and decided I'm not worth the trouble." She hoped that was the case, but then she might never know who was behind it, and that was even worse.

"It's possible he's grown bored of messing with you. Do you think the police will let it go if nothing more happens?"

She shrugged. "I don't know." An idea struck her. "What are you doing this afternoon?"

"The norm. Grading papers, entering grades, then heading home. Why?"

"I thought we could grab a cup of coffee. My treat. A thank you for judging the finalists."

He raised a brow. "I'd like that, but aren't you and Titus seeing each other?"

"We went out once." He'd not asked her out since, and for whatever reason she felt compelled to ask Luke to coffee—she'd only used his help as an excuse.

"I have a few things to finish up. Meet me in my

room in twenty minutes?"

"Sure." She watched him leave then leaned back and closed her eyes. What had come over her? She never asked men to coffee! And said man was Luke not Titus. She finally knew what she had to do. She squared her shoulders and marched to Titus's office. She stopped outside his door. "Hey, there. Glad I caught you. Do you have a minute?"

"Of course. Come in."

She closed the door and took a seat. "I owe you an apology."

"For what?"

"The thing is I like you as a friend, but that's all we can be."

"I see." He stood and walked around to the front of his desk.

Her heart thundered, and she stood. "Please don't be angry."

He leaned against his desk. "I'm not. Actually, I appreciate you stopping by. I wondered what had happened between us. We'd seemed to be headed one direction then all of a sudden we weren't."

"I know. Nothing happened really except I think I was using you to feed my ego and make me feel safe. That's not a good foundation for a relationship."

His brows rose. "Feed your ego?"

"Yeah, well, you're quite the catch."

He grinned wide. "And you're very good at letting people down gently."

She chuckled. "I'm a nervous wreck."

He laughed. "I couldn't tell." He thrust out his hand. "Friends?"

She grasped his hand. "Absolutely. Thanks for

being there for me."

"You bet. I'm always here if you need anything."

"I appreciate that. I'll catch you later."

He walked beside her to his door and pulled it open. "See you."

She ambled back to her room feeling a lot lighter with that conversation behind her. Granted, she still carried the weight of the trouble she was dealing with, but at least she no longer had to fret about Titus.

Luke walked into Roaster's Coffee with Anna by his side. He still couldn't believe she'd asked him to coffee. Sure, she'd said it was a thank you for judging, but it felt like more than that. "What're you getting?"

"I'm thinking about herbal tea. It's too late in the day for caffeine."

He wrinkled his nose. He'd never acquired a taste for tea.

She chuckled. "You don't approve?"

"I don't care for it myself. I'm more of a coffee man."

She grinned. "Place your order, and I'll pay."

"I can get our drinks."

"Nope. This is my thank you. I'm paying." She pulled out her wallet, clearly not willing to budge on the issue.

He ordered a medium iced coffee. A few minutes later they sat by the window. He took a long draw from the straw. "Maddie tells me the book club is growing."

Anna's eyes sparkled. "Yes. Three more students joined this month. It's fun to see their enthusiasm for reading spread. I'm proud of Maddie and Gavin for the work they put into not only choosing the books and running the club, but the extra effort they've put into promoting it."

"That's my little girl. She doesn't do anything halfway." He couldn't have stopped smiling if he'd wanted to. Maddie was growing into a responsible young woman, in spite of his lack of stellar parenting skills, but he had made great progress these past few months.

"I've noticed that about her. She has a lot of potential, and I predict she will do great things in life."

He sat up a little taller. "Thanks. I'm going to encourage her to enter the writing contest next year—another reason I didn't want to be in charge anymore."

"I didn't think about that, but since the entries are blind, it shouldn't be an issue if you end up judging."

Luke shook his head. "I'd rather be safe than sorry. I feel like I'd recognize her writing."

"I suppose that's possible. Thanks for offering to do the final round. I'm ready to be done with the whole thing."

"I understand." He felt for her and all the trouble this contest had caused. "By next year though, the students should be more accepting of a new coordinator."

"If there is a next year for me."

He raised his brows. "Why do you say that? Are you leaving Tipton High School?"

"Not by choice, but as you know, Ms. Porter is not

letting that cheating accusation drop. Plus, she's angry with me about the rat, and I feel like she's using the cheating accusation to get back at me."

"Then we need to pray that she doesn't succeed." He wanted to deny the truth of her words but couldn't. Ms. Porter wanted to retire without scandal, and Anna's situation had marred her perfect record as principal of Tipton High.

Anna tipped her head to the side. "You're right. For the second time today, I've been reminded that I need to follow my own advice."

"And what would that be?" He leaned forward slightly.

"Prayer. One of my students came to me with a relationship problem awhile back and then again today. She's a Christian and makes no secret of her faith. Because of that, I felt comfortable advising her to pray for guidance." A gentle smile touched her lips.

"What?" He smiled back, mesmerized by her beautiful green eyes. He was finally able to move on from his wife's death. His heart hammered. The truth of his growing feelings walloped him over the head—but to what end if she didn't feel the same? He was more than likely setting himself up for heartbreak. How much more could he take? He needed to tread carefully.

"She asked me what to do if she didn't like the Lord's answer."

His mouth opened slightly before he closed it. Whoever this student was, she had wisdom beyond her years. So often when he prayed he expected to get the answer he wanted—he didn't even consider the possibility of being told no or otherwise. "She sounds like a wise young woman."

Anna shrugged. "In some ways. In other ways, not so much. She got mixed up with a guy who was pressuring her to take their relationship further than she was comfortable with. She dumped him, but now she's considering getting back with him."

"I wouldn't be so quick to judge. The heart does what it wants." He knew that firsthand. "Wisdom might still reign."

Her eyes widened, and a smile quivered on her lips.

"You think that's funny?" Surprise filled his voice.

"Not at all. I'm pleasantly surprised. You're a romantic. I never would have guessed. Then again, maybe I should've since you brought me flowers."

His face heated. "My mom loved flowers and thought they were good for any occasion." His wife had too.

"Mm-hmm. Whatever you say. But I'm onto you. You're a romantic at heart." Her eyes twinkled.

He shrugged and reached for his iced coffee—anything to cool the heat that suddenly gripped his body. He took a long draw from the straw then rested the cup back on the table, keeping his hands wrapped around it, willing the cold to seep through his body. He wasn't one to blush, but what Anna thought of him mattered—a lot. Then again… "There's nothing wrong with being a romantic."

"I didn't suggest there was." She leaned her elbows on the table, lacing her fingers together and resting her chin on them, and grinned. "I'm pleasantly surprised by this discovery." She sobered and sat back. "But I didn't mean to embarrass you.

I'm sorry for that."

She must have finally noticed he was flushed—at least he felt as red as a cherry. Hmm, it seemed Anna was feeling a little embarrassed too since her face had turned a pretty, soft pink. "It's fine...I'm fine."

Anna averted her gaze then sat back and reached for her tea and sipped it. She finally looked back at him. "I'll forward the finalist entries to you when I get home."

Ah, back to business. It was probably for the best. "Sounds good. I'll keep an eye out for them." He finished off his iced coffee. "Thanks for this. I should head home."

"You're welcome. I'm going to sit a while. I'll see you."

He nodded and stood then headed for the door. He glanced over his shoulder before walking out the door and caught her watching him. She ducked her chin and jerked her head forward. Hope squeezed his chest as he left. Anna was a mystery. He'd always enjoyed a good mystery. But would he get burned trying to solve this one?

Chapter Nineteen

NANCY LACED FINGERS WITH CARTER AS they strolled along the sidewalk in downtown Tipton. Sunshine matched her mood. She could think of no better way to spend a Sunday afternoon. "I believe I'm close to figuring out who is behind all of Anna's trouble."

"Really?" He glanced at her. "Care to share?"

"Not yet." She needed to follow up with an idea first.

He frowned.

"Ah, come on. Don't be like that, Carter. You know how I hate to be wrong. I need to make sure before I say anything."

He sighed "There's nothing wrong with bouncing an idea off of me, even if you're not right."

"There is if you act on it and someone gets hurt." She shook her head. "I need to make certain I'm on the right track, then I'll let you know." It was no secret her personality quirk frustrated him, but she'd rather have him frustrated than dead. Besides, she didn't want to sully a person's name. She still espoused innocent until proven guilty—no longer the norm, but she believed it was the right way to do things. Accusations, false or not had a way of sticking.

"Nancy, you need to learn to trust me."

"I do trust you." How could he even think that?

"No, you don't. If you did, you'd tell me what's going on in your head and trust me to deal with the information responsibly."

She frowned. Was he right? She released his hand. "If what you say is true, it's unconscious. As far as trust goes, you're at the top of my list."

He draped his arm across her shoulder. "I'm glad to hear that. What time will your mom and Lyle be over for dinner?"

"Not until this evening. I know a lot of people do an early meal on Sundays, but I wanted to have you to myself for a while."

"I like that." He lightly squeezed her shoulder. "What are we having for dinner?"

She grinned. "You wouldn't happen to be hungry?"

"Guilty."

"The BLB is ahead. You want to grab something there?"

"Might be a good idea. I don't think I'll make it three more hours."

She spotted Titus's truck across the street. It looked like he might be exercising his dog at the park. "How about you go get something to eat, and while you're there, I'll wait in the park? I need to talk to Titus."

He frowned. "Why not come in and wait with me then we can go say hi together?"

"Because it's too sunny and beautiful to be inside." She stopped at the entrance. "Go on. I want to soak in some vitamin D."

He huffed a breath and went inside. At least he hadn't pushed the issue. She looked both ways then rushed across the street. As she'd expected, Titus and his dog were there.

She tucked her hands into the pockets of her

lightweight jacket and strolled up the grassy knoll to where they played. "Hey, there."

Titus looked her way and grinned. "Hi, Nancy. Long time no see."

"I was thinking the same. I haven't seen you around the neighborhood."

He frowned. "I've been busy."

"I understand. The contest winner will be announced tomorrow, and Anna and I are hoping whoever is behind her trouble won't be an issue after that." At least she hoped that was the case, but if her latest theory was correct, the contest had nothing to do with Anna's trouble.

"I was under the impression her trouble had stopped."

Nancy shrugged. She didn't want to give him any information if Anna wasn't keeping him updated—it wasn't hers to share. Besides that, she was hoping to learn something new. Anything that would aid in the investigation would be welcome. After all, he knew the students at the school better than she did. "Nothing's happened in the past few days, but until the person is caught and Anna's name is cleared, I'm encouraging her to stay at my place."

"I'm glad to hear that. I was concerned about her being alone. You're a good friend and neighbor."

"Do you mind if I pick your brain?"

He tossed a tennis ball, and his dog loped after it. "Go for it."

"I'm running with a new idea. Based on the evidence, it appears the boy or boys behind Anna's trouble are underclassmen. That doesn't jibe with the contest theory."

His body stiffened, and his gaze shot her way. "Go on." His dog dropped to his belly and rested nearby.

"I've been able to narrow down my list of suspects to two boys. James Jensen and Jordan Black."

A troubled look rested on Titus's face. "I can't imagine either of those boys being involved. I thought the police cleared them?"

"They did, but these two still bother me."

"Why?"

"We know they would have been in the PE class where Gavin overheard some boys talking about getting back at Anna, and that they were listed as being present in class. We also know they both have her for English. So maybe one of them didn't like a grade he received, and that's what set all of this into motion. It could have been a coincidence that it started when Anna took over the contest."

"Hmm. I suppose so. I assume they're on your list because their grades aren't good?"

She nodded. "They both have a D."

"That's odd since they are usually A students. I'll look into it."

"Thanks." She grinned. Movement along the perimeter of the park grabbed her attention. "Looks like Carter got his burger. Please keep our conversation between you and me."

"Carter doesn't know what you're thinking?"

"No, and I want to keep it that way. He doesn't like that I won't let this go, and he'll just tell me they've already been cleared."

He frowned but nodded.

"Thanks." She turned and waved to Carter then headed his way. "What'd you get?"

"A cheeseburger."

Her stomach rumbled. Maybe skipping lunch had been a bad idea. "Let's head back to my place. I need to get dinner prepared and into the oven." Good thing she'd planned to make a salad. She could snag a few veggies as she made it.

"What were you and Titus talking about?"

"I asked why we hadn't seen him around. I thought he was into Anna. You know they went out once?"

He nodded as he tossed the last bite of his burger into his mouth. "He mentioned it."

"Anna was non-committal regarding him. I figured she was being coy, but it looks like he's really not into her. I sure thought he was though."

Carter chuckled. "Since when did you become a matchmaker?"

"I'm not matchmaking. But my powers of observation are certainly off."

Nancy sat across from her mom and Carter while Lyle sat beside her. She figured it would work best for conversation to have the "couples" across from one another.

"The roast smells wonderful." Her mom looked like she might salivate any second.

"Thanks. Carter, would you bless the food?"

Everyone bowed their heads as he said a short prayer. After he said amen, she glanced up and their gazes locked. Her heart skipped at the look in his eyes. Her mom's prediction that there'd be a proposal forthcoming by January played in her mind. Granted, she'd said it way back in October, and January had come and gone, but if she could believe the look in Carter's eyes then...

"You okay, Nancy?" Lyle nudged her arm with his elbow.

She shook off her thoughts. "I'm fine. Did I miss something?"

Her mom chuckled. "Nothing much." She passed Nancy the salad. "Lyle said that he thought they were close to wrapping up Anna's case."

Nancy's breath caught as she shifted in her seat to face him. "Did you find new evidence?"

Lyle shook his head. "No. But the contest winner will be announced tomorrow during an assembly. The way I see it, if her trouble is related to it, then the person will be revealed."

"But what if the contest has nothing to do with it? And how would they be revealed? Unless you think they're going to flip out."

He frowned. "All the evidence supports our hypothesis that the two are related. If anyone seems to be acting up or threatens Anna in any way we'll move in."

"No disrespect meant, but we are talking about teenagers. I don't know how you can look at one and say he's the troublemaker. Plus, I'm not convinced the writing contest has anything to do with it. The boys who Gavin overheard in the locker room are sophomores. They aren't even eligible for the contest."

"I'm aware, but they were cleared. When I interviewed them, one of the boys admitted to running off at the mouth, but it had to do with a grade she'd given him. He was angry and venting. You're forgetting the graffiti targeted the homes of the high school English teachers."

"They could have done that to throw us off," Nancy said.

"We don't think so." Lyle cut through a slice of roast and took a bite. "Mmm. It's as good as it smells."

"Thanks." Nancy ran through what Lyle had just said and caught her breath. "Oh. I wish you would have told me the boys were angry about a grade. I surmised that was the case, but it would've been nice to have been told." She looked at Carter.

Her mom cleared her throat. "I'm afraid that's my fault. Please don't take this the wrong way, but after what happened this past fall, I'm not okay with you poking around in a police investigation."

This was the first time her mom had bluntly stated what Nancy had suspected for the past several months—her time as a police consultant was over. "I see. Anna is my friend, and she's asked me to help figure this out."

"There's no law against that," her mom said. "But I've asked my deputies to stop giving you updates."

Carter mouthed *sorry*. Acid rose in her throat. How long had he been keeping things from her? "You could've told me."

"I tried," Carter said. "You wouldn't listen."

She huffed a breath then filled half of her plate with salad. She would not ruin what was supposed to be a fun meal with her favorite people. But to be fair, now that she thought about it, Carter had probably told her more than her mother wanted, so she wouldn't hold this against him.

"Thanks for inviting me over, Nancy. A home cooked meal that consists of food not cooked in the microwave is a rare treat." Lyle took another bite of the roast.

"You're welcome. It's a treat for me to have all of you here together." She would not allow police business to ruin their meal. After all, she'd invited them because she thought Lyle and her mom should socialize outside of work. She had a feeling there would be a spark if one was allowed to ignite. Too bad they weren't cooperating. So far the dinner wasn't going at all like she'd hoped.

Mom sent her a questioning glance. Nancy held back a grin and instead shot her a blank look. Her mother would be livid if she knew why Nancy had invited Lyle over. "It's supposed to be nice weather this week. I'm thinking of going to the coast to watch the sunset. Anyone else care to join me?" Okay, maybe that was too much.

"Count me in," Carter said.

Nancy looked to her mom and Lyle. "How about the two of you?"

Mom's eyes widened then narrowed. It looked like she'd figured out what Nancy was up to. "I'll pass, but thanks for the invite."

"I'm going to pass too. I'm not a fan of the coast—too cold."

"Your loss." This matchmaking was a lot more difficult than she'd expected. It'd probably be best to stick to sleuthing. At least that was something she was semi-good at—plus, it was fun. Matchmaking not so much. And no matter what Lyle said about being close to wrapping up Anna's case, she would keep at it.

Not long after the meal Lyle and her mother left. She faced Carter. "That was a bust."

"What are you talking about? I thought the meal was great."

"Thanks, but I meant my mom and Lyle. I was hoping there'd be a spark."

"There's a spark right here." He chuckled and drew her to him. Wrapping his arms around her waist, he looked down at her. "Is that what the coast sunset was about?"

She nodded.

"You can't force love, Nancy."

"I know." She slid her hands up his chest and rested them there. His heart beat steady against the palm of her hand. "But they are perfect for each other."

"Perfect or not, they have to agree."

She blew out a breath. "I know."

"Good." He lowered his face and captured her mouth with his in a sweet and gentle kiss that was over too soon. "I love how your mind works." He caressed the space between her shoulder blades. "Though I also love kissing you senseless."

"You're welcome to admire my brain anytime." She shot him a coy smile. "As for the kisses..." She rose up slightly and pecked his lips. "You're welcome to those anytime too."

"I like the sound of that." He placed feather-light kisses down her neck, stopping at her shoulder. "I should go."

She sighed. "Okay. When Anna gets back, I'm

going to find out the time of the assembly at the high school. I want to be there when the winner is announced."

"It's at nine."

"I should've known you'd know." She stepped out of his embrace. "Maybe I'll see you there."

"Perhaps." He took her hand and gave it a squeeze before leaving.

Nancy grabbed her phone and sent Anna a text, letting her know that everyone had left. Anna chose to hang out at her own house for the day but would spend the night like she'd been doing. As much as Nancy wanted to be the one to solve the mystery of who was behind the angry notes and the trouble Anna had been receiving, she would be happy if the police solved it first. All she wanted was for her friend to be out of danger.

Chapter Twenty

LUKE STOOD ON THE GYM FLOOR with a microphone in his hands. A side door opened and someone wheeled Zander into the gym and parked him beside the bleachers. A hush came over the school and all eyes were trained on the young man who'd cheated death. But he couldn't escape his legal troubles. He'd heard through the grapevine that Zander was facing reckless driving charges as well as a couple of other charges. "Welcome back, Zander."

Zander raised the arm not in a cast and waved to his classmates. An awkward silence filled the gym.

Luke cleared his throat. "As most of you know, we hold a writing contest each year in memory of Melinda Stephens. Will the following students please come forward? Entry numbers twenty-two, three, and thirty-nine. Make sure you bring proof of your entry number with you." It hadn't been the plan for him to do this, but Anna was so nervous, he'd offered to do the presentation.

A slight commotion ensued as two girls and a boy made their way over to him. He confirmed their entries then faced the bleachers where the entire school waited to learn the recipient of the Melinda Stephens Literary Scholarship. "I present to you this years' finalists. Tiffany Smith, Jake Simmons, and Shelby Trask."

Applause and whistles burst through the

gymnasium. He raised a hand to silence them after a long minute. "The winner of the scholarship is Shelby Trask. Congratulations!"

Luke presented Shelby with a certificate and an award letter—he'd add her name after the assembly. They posed for a yearbook picture then he passed the microphone to Ms. Porter.

Plainclothes deputies stood near the exits. He'd spotted Nancy near the top of the bleachers. Anna sat in the front row—worry etched her brow. He sat beside her and offered a reassuring smile. "You okay?" He asked through the side of his mouth.

"I'm nervous."

"It's going to be okay." He wanted to wrap his hand over hers but knew it would be frowned on if their boss noticed—and she had zeroed in on them.

"I would like to thank Miss Plum for running the writing contest this year and Mr. Harms for judging the final round." Ms. Porter led the school in a polite applause.

Luke waved a hand, grabbed Anna's, and stood. "Take a bow."

The students got louder and whistled then whoops ensued. He tugged her toward the exit. Once outside the gym she pulled her hand free.

"Why did you do that?" Confusion filled her eyes.

"I wanted to get you out of there in case whoever has been threatening you had plans."

"Oh." Her face softened. "That was really sweet. Thank you. With the police presence, plain clothes or not, I don't think anyone would try anything today. Everyone in this town knows the cops."

"True." They didn't have much time before the

assembly let out. Student leadership had selected kids from each grade to compete against one another in a silly game and then they would be flooding through the doors. "How about we head to your room to avoid the stampede?"

She nodded and moved forward.

"I was pleasantly surprised by who the finalists were," Luke said.

"Me too. I had all of them in my class when they were sophomores, but their writing skills don't stand out in my mind."

"We've been working a lot on it this year." As the senior class English teacher, he considered it his duty to make sure they were prepared for college level writing.

Anna pulled on the door to her room and propped it open. "I don't know why I thought everything would go back to normal after the assembly today."

Luke followed her into the room. "What makes you think it won't? The contest is done. The student can no longer do anything to try and influence the outcome."

Anna turned to face him and leaned against her desk, crossing her arms. "Did you know Nancy doesn't believe the contest has anything to do with it? In fact, she thinks they're unrelated."

He sat on a nearby desk and rubbed his clean-shaven chin. "She could be right, but that doesn't explain the graffiti."

"Maybe he was trying to throw us off."

"Maybe he is really a she." He raised a brow.

"You're doing a lot to ease my mind." She shot him a nervous smile.

He chuckled. "I'm sorry. How about you come over to my place tonight? Maddie and Gavin will be there. I'll pick up takeout and we can watch a movie."

"On a Monday night?" She scrunched her nose.

"What? You don't eat takeout on Mondays?"

She laughed. "I've been known to, but I generally stay in on Mondays."

The sound of nearby voices registered in his mind. He stood. "I'll explain the benefit of a relaxing Monday evening out later. I need to go unlock my classroom. Come by my room after school?" He waited for her response.

A mix of emotions played across her face then she grinned. "Sure. Now scat. I have a class to teach."

He turned, nearly bumping into a student. "Excuse me." He left with a little spring to his step. She hadn't said yes, but he knew she would. The look of interest in her eyes was difficult to miss even if her words said otherwise.

"Are you sure you don't mind me leaving Freddy here?" Anna stood with her hand on the front doorknob to Nancy's house. She was supposed to be at Luke's five minutes ago—good thing he lived nearby. She'd shot him a text to let him know she was running a few minutes late.

"Stop worrying, Anna. Freddy and I are buddies. Have fun tonight."

"Okay. Thanks. I seriously owe you." She pulled open the door then darted to her car. She squatted beside the front passenger wheel and ran her finger along a gash. Someone had slashed her tire. She stood and inspected the rest. Tears of frustration burned the rims of her eyes. "Nancy!"

Her friend rushed outside with Freddy at her heels. "What's wrong?"

"All my tires are slashed. You have video surveillance, right?"

Nancy grinned. "I sure do."

With any luck they'd finally know who was behind all her trouble. She pulled out her cell phone again, but this time she called Luke. "Hey, I have a problem. All my tires are slashed."

"You're kidding! I can come get you."

She hesitated. Shouldn't she stick around and view the video?

Nancy waved a hand. "Let him come and get you. I'll pull the video feed and text you with what I find."

"Hold on a second, Luke." She muted the phone. "What about calling the police and filing a report?"

"I'll do that too. It happened in my driveway, on my property."

Anna hesitated. Should she allow Nancy to deal with this on her own? Sure, she said she would, but this was her problem, not Nancy's.

"I know that look," Nancy said. "I have an in with the police in Tipton. It's no problem for me to deal with this." She grinned with a mischievous look in her eyes. "I'm hoping that Carter is sent over to write up the report."

Anna nodded, unmuted the phone. "Luke?"

"I'm here."

"I'll be waiting."

"Sounds good. I'm almost to your place. I headed out when you put me on hold. Please wait for me inside."

"Okay. See you soon." Anna pocketed her phone. "He wants me to wait inside."

"Good thinking. This punk might be nearby watching."

Anna shivered at the thought. "I'm never going to be able to repay you for all you've done for me." She followed Nancy into the house.

"Pfff. Don't mention it. I'm kind of excited it happened here. Clearly they don't realize I have a surveillance system in place."

Anna heard a car's engine and glanced out the window. "That's Luke. Call me when you know something."

"I will." Nancy waved as she left the room.

Torn between wanting to watch over her friend's shoulder and spending the evening with Luke, she stood there.

A knock sounded. She opened the door. "Thanks for coming to get me." With a fleeting glance in the direction Nancy had gone, she left with Luke.

He rested a hand in the middle of her back. "I saw your tires. I'd really hoped this would end after the winner was announced this morning."

"Me too."

He opened the passenger door for her. She sat and buckled in as he closed the door then went around and eased in beside her. "I told the kids to start eating without us."

"That's fine. I'm sorry about this."

"Don't be. It's not your fault."

"Maybe it is." Unease nipped at her. "I did something to cause this kind of behavior."

"You are not responsible for someone else's actions." He reached out and gave her hand a quick squeeze then put it back on the steering wheel.

Anna's hand tingled from his touch. "Thanks for the encouragement. I realize everyone is responsible for their own actions, but it seems to me, something I said or did set this person off. I have a bad feeling things are only going to get worse until he or she is found and stopped." His silence unnerved her—he clearly agreed. She'd been hoping for an argument. She swallowed the lump that had formed in her throat and took a shaky breath. "I'm scared."

He pulled to the curb in front of his house and parked. "You have a right to be, but I don't think this punk would actually hurt you. He seems to get off on nuisance crimes and threats."

"True, but that doesn't make me feel much better. Nancy is a bit of a surveillance freak. I'm hoping the person was caught on video, and we'll be able to identify them. She's checking now."

"Good."

A text message pinged on her phone. She raised her phone. "It was a single male wearing a dark hoodie. He kept his face down the entire time. Sending this to Carter."

"Sounds like progress."

"I agree," Anna said. "Can you believe I'm hungry? I kind of lost my appetite when I discovered my tires slashed, but Nancy's message gives me renewed hope."

He chuckled, hopped out, then went around to

her side and opened her door. "I hope you don't mind pizza again."

"Nope." She took his proffered hand to help her out. He released it when they started toward the house. Awareness filled her—this was the spark she'd missed with Titus. She shot a quick glance toward Luke.

"What?" His brow rose.

"Mmm, nothing. Just a thought I had surprised me."

"O-kay," he drew out the word. "Care to share?"

"I don't think so." She lowered her chin as her face heated.

One corner of his lip curved up as he pushed open his front door. "We're here."

"I don't think I've ever been inside your place." She glanced from the entryway to the tired looking house. She suspected it resembled a time capsule from when his wife had died. Given the same circumstances, she probably wouldn't have wasted energy on her home either.

"It's not much, but it's comfortable. I'll give you the grand tour later if you'd like. Food's in the kitchen." He led the way.

On second look, all the house really needed was a fresh coat of paint, and updated furniture. Otherwise it wasn't so bad.

Luke stopped beside the kitchen island. "Grab a plate. There's plenty, so eat up."

"Thanks. Where are the kids?"

"Good question. I think I'd better figure that out. Be back in a minute."

As soon as he left the room, a back door opened.

Maddie stood in the doorway and stifled a scream. "Miss Plum, you scared me."

Gavin laughed. "You jump at everything."

"Your dad's looking for you." Anna picked up a piece of cheese pizza and placed it on a plate.

"Dad! We're in the kitchen," Maddie shouted then reached for a slice with the works and sat on a stool at the island. "My dad told us about your tires."

"Yeah. I can't wait until this kid is caught," Anna said.

Gavin washed his hands. "My uncle said the same thing the other day. He's frustrated that no one ever sees him or that the IT people weren't able to track him down from his computer signature or whatever it's called."

Anna frowned. Whoever this kid was, he was good, but the authorities had to be better. "He didn't get that lucky this time. Nancy caught him on her surveillance camera." Anna grinned and bit into her pizza.

"Does this mean they're going to stop him?" Maddie asked.

Anna crumpled the napkin in her hand. "I don't know. It depends on if they can identify him. Nancy's showing the police the video now."

"Cool," Gavin said. "I hope they get him."

Luke traipsed into the kitchen. "Where were you?"

Maddie motioned toward the backyard. "I wanted to show Gavin where we're going to put the garden. He said he'd help."

"That's nice of you, Gavin." Luke washed his hands. "Do you enjoy gardening?"

Gavin shrugged. "Beats me. I've never tried."

"Lauren was looking for you after school," Maddie said. "Did she find you?"

Anna nodded. "I didn't know you were friends."

"We're not close, but we're in the same youth group at church."

"I see. Do you know her old boyfriend?"

She wrinkled her nose. "Unfortunately."

Luke placed three slices of pizza onto a plate and sat beside Anna at the island. "Who are we talking about, and why don't you like him?"

"Isaac Bugler. I don't dislike him, but Lauren told me a little bit about what was going on between them and why she broke up with him. Guys like that make me angry."

"Me too." Luke said "Is there more?

She shook her head. "You don't want to know." Her face heated at the thought of explaining the situation to him in front of the kids.

He frowned but thankfully didn't push it. "Since it's a school night we should get the movie started. We can eat while we watch it."

"I chose a classic," Maddie said. "Breakfast at Tiffany's."

"Sounds fine with me." Luke followed after his daughter.

Anna caught the look of distaste on Gavin's face before he shuttered it. She held in a chuckle. If she didn't know better, she'd think he had a crush on Maddie.

Anna slid a second piece of pizza onto her plate, filled a cup with ice-cold water then carried her meal into the family room and sat on the sofa beside Luke. She hadn't seen this movie in at least a decade. It had never been a favorite, but she adored Audrey Hepburn.

When the credits scrolled on the screen, Luke flicked off the television. He motioned toward Gavin who slept soundly in a recliner.

"What did you think?" Maddie turned from her position on the floor where she was laying, propped up by pillows. She frowned when she looked at Gavin then tossed a pillow at him.

Gavin's eyes flew open. "I'm up."

They all laughed.

"Not your kind of movie?" Luke stood and stretched. "Not mine either. The guys get to choose next time."

"I suppose that's fair." Maddie stood and tossed the rest of the pillows she'd been using onto the couch. "Is your uncle coming to get you?"

"Yeah. He said to text." Gavin pulled out his phone.

Anna followed Luke into the kitchen. "Thanks for tonight. In spite of my tires being slashed, I managed to have fun." She meant it too. Being here with Luke and his daughter had been a treat. Come to think of it, she'd had more fun than the time they'd come to her place for pizza and a movie—that night still held mixed emotions for her. They were in their element at their own house, and she'd enjoyed listening to their banter, though infrequent, during the movie.

Tonight had taken an interesting twist, and for the first time in a long while, she felt like everything was going to be okay.

Chapter Twenty-One

PUMPING HER ARMS, NANCY STRODE beside Anna. "I know my news was disappointing." When she'd told Anna the video of the kid slashing her tires hadn't turned up a solid lead, she'd left out that the police had uploaded the recording to Facebook and it had gone viral. If she knew one thing for certain, it was that social media helped catch criminals.

"Definitely disappointing."

"Keep in mind that just because they couldn't get a solid lead, doesn't mean it's a dead end."

"I don't see why not." Anna shook her head. "I don't want to talk about this anymore today. I would like a trouble-free, relaxing walk."

"I understand your feelings. I'd want the same. Let's talk about Luke instead."

Anna clicked her tongue. "How about we talk about you and Carter."

Nancy chuckled. Clearly that topic was off limits. "What about us?"

"Ever since your accident, something has changed between the two of you. By the way, how are you feeling?"

"Much better. Just a little stiff. And you're right about Carter. My accident shook him up. I think he might actually propose soon." She still wasn't sure how she felt about it. Yes, she loved him, but marriage was a huge commitment.

Anna grasped her arm and pulled her to a stop. "I'm so excited for you. Any idea when he's going to pop the question?"

"Not a clue, but he did ask me out for this coming Saturday."

A dreamy look filled Anna's eyes. "You will make the most beautiful bride."

"Oh, stop. He hasn't even asked me." Nancy's cheeks heated. She never should have said anything about a possible proposal.

"Yet."

"Right."

"I have a confession to make." Anna ducked her chin and resumed walking. "I'm jealous."

"Oh, sweetie. I'm sorry. I didn't mean to make you feel bad. Your day is coming."

"Maybe." Anna shrugged. "I don't know. For a while I thought I was interested in Titus, then something changed. Maybe I'm the one who changed. I like him as a friend and enjoy hanging out with him, but there wasn't really a spark. You know what I mean?"

"I think so. But you were attracted to him, weren't you?"

"I was. He's a great guy, but I don't know, it didn't feel right. I broke it off with him. Not that there was anything official to break off, but...well it seemed like the right thing to do."

"You should definitely listen to your instincts. I think the Lord gives us those for a reason. In my opinion, it's one of His ways to communicate with us."

"Interesting theory." Anna slowed. "I've been thinking a lot about Luke. He seems interested, but he's a hard man to read. I can't tell if he's only being nice, or if he's being nice because he has feelings for me."

Nancy adjusted her pace to match Anna's. "I can't say with absolute certainty, but I think it's probably safe to say the man is interested. I don't think he would have dropped everything to go and pick up just anyone like he did for you the other night."

Anna chuckled. "Now that you mention it, he wouldn't have. At least, I don't think so."

"Based on what you've told me about him, I know so. However, he sure has transformed."

"No kidding. He's like the man he used to be before his wife's death. I liked him back then." She shook her head. "That came out wrong. I liked who he was as a person, not that I had feelings for him."

Nancy grinned. "I understood." She motioned toward the park. "You want to let Freddy run? We can rest a bit on a bench." She wouldn't admit it out loud, but her body needed a break. That accident had taken a toll on her. In addition to her walks with Anna, she'd been either walking or hitching rides to work. She really needed to get a new car, but how could she ever replace her classic?

"Resting sounds nice, and I'm sure Freddy will love the freedom. He's been doing so much better at not running off. I give you credit for that."

Nancy smiled. The little rascal had always been a handful, but since Anna had been staying with her, he'd calmed. He probably only needed the extra attention having two people in the house gave him. She stopped at the bench closest to the off-leash dog area and sat.

Anna released Freddy. He sniffed the grass around them, then plopped down onto his belly panting. Anna chuckled. "Looks like we tired him out."

"I didn't know that was possible."

Chuckling, Anna joined her on the bench and sighed. "I haven't been completely forthcoming."

Her curiosity piqued, she shifted to face Anna.

"A conversation with a student not all that long ago reminded me that I need to pray about my relationships, and that regardless of His answer, I need to obey."

"That's a deep conversation to have with a student."

Anna retied her shoes. "Lauren is that kind of person. She'd been seeing a guy who was pressuring her for sex, and she came to me for advice. She goes to my church, so I asked her what the Bible said. She knew what she should do without being told. I think she only needed to have an impartial sounding board."

"So she broke up with him?"

"Yes. But then he wouldn't leave her alone, and that's when we talked about prayer and obedience. I think she really likes him and was about to give in."

"Any idea what happened?"

Anna shook her head. "No. She's a senior, so I really only see her if she seeks me out."

"Who's the guy?"

Anna frowned. "Isaac Bugler."

"When did she first approach you about this guy?"

"Goodness, over a month ago. Why?"

Excitement bubbled through Nancy. "We need to find out if they got back together."

"I don't see that it's any of our business."

"It might not be, but I have a hunch." She stood with renewed energy. "Come on. Let's go find this girl."

"What? No." Anna stayed planted on the bench and crossed her arms.

"Why not?" Nancy rested her hands at her hips.

"For starters, seeking out a student outside of school is against school policy. If she comes to me to ask for advice, that's one thing, but for me to show up at her home is quite another. After the whole cheating thing, something like this would destroy my career. No one would ever hire me again, and I'd probably make the evening news."

Nancy rolled her eyes. "I had no idea you could be so melodramatic."

"I'm not. This is my reality. I'm sorry, but unless she comes to me…"

Nancy plopped back onto the bench. "My instinct tells me to pursue this. At least give me the girl's last name so I can look her up. I'm not bound by school policy, so I can talk to her."

Anna looked off to the distance and seemed to be debating. She returned her focus to Nancy. "She trusts me."

"I won't mention you gave me her name."

"She'll know."

"Not necessarily. Maybe her boyfriend talked to me. She would have no way of knowing."

Anna closed her eyes for a moment then opened them. "Fine. Her name is Lauren Jones."

"Is she the Lauren that's in Luke's English class?"

"He'd be her teacher since she's a senior."

Yes! "I know her. She introduced herself the day I did a talk about the summer reading program at the library." Nancy grabbed Freddy's leash from beside Anna and clipped it to the dog. "Let's go."

Anna looked at her warily. "Where are we going?"

"Home." If her suspicion was correct, the troublemaker bothering Anna would soon be in police custody.

The day after her unsettling talk with Nancy, Anna weeded in her backyard. Freddy romped nearby after a butterfly. Normally the site would make her laugh, but today she was on edge. If Nancy's hunch was correct then the mess her life had turned into would soon turn back to normal.

The sound of her gate latch clicking made her jump. She tensed and looked over her shoulder. The gate inched open. "Luke! You nearly scared me half to death."

"Sorry. Nancy said you were over here. I rang your bell, but you didn't answer, so I figured I'd see if you were out back."

She stood and pulled her gloves off one finger at a time and set them aside. "What brings you by?" Her pulse still beat a rapid staccato, but it wasn't from the initial surprise of seeing him enter her yard unexpectedly.

"I missed seeing you at school today." He strolled toward her patio and sat in one of her chairs.

His words sent a jolt through her. She'd been praying a lot about her feelings for him and had come to the conclusion she had the Lord's blessing to see where things led. She joined Luke and sat in one facing him. "I had a full day and then the book club met after school. Did you need something?" She reminded herself to breathe.

"Not really." He looked away. "Have you heard from Ms. Porter regarding the investigation?"

She shook her head. "I've been doing my best to not think about it." Besides Nancy's sleuthing had taken front and center in her mind since yesterday. If anyone asked her what book they'd discussed in the club today she wouldn't be able to tell them since her mind had been far from the room.

"Then I'm sorry for mentioning it." He stared off toward the back-fence line for a moment then turned to face her. "The thing is, I like you, and to be honest I haven't been interested in another woman since my wife's death. I'm out of practice." He ran a hand through his hair. "I'm sure this isn't as awkward for you as it is for me." He cleared his throat. "What I'm trying to say is—I really like you, Anna, and I'd like to date you. That is if there's no one else in your life." His gaze met hers. "What do you think?"

His soulful, green eyes turned her to mush. "I'd like that too. And there's no one else in my life."

His eyes widened. "Really? I thought...I mean. Great!"

She giggled like a schoolgirl, certain her face matched the pink cherry blossom flowers in the tree at the far end of her yard. She cleared her throat. "Yes. I like you, Luke. I've enjoyed seeing the old you transform into this new you. I like the new you a lot."

He grinned. "Thanks. I like who I am now too. If I was a turkey to you during my years of self-pity, anger, and grief, I am truly sorry."

She waved a hand. "Ancient history. Besides, I believe you've already apologized. Not to be pushy or anything, but when did you want to start this dating thing?"

He laughed. "How about this Friday night? And for the record, we have my daughter's blessing."

Unexplainable peace washed over her. "Friday is perfect."

"Great!" He stood. "Want help weeding?"

Her eyes widened. No one ever volunteered to help her with yard work. "That's very sweet, but I only have one pair of gloves."

"I don't need gloves, but if you'd rather, I could mow the grass." His eyes crinkled at the edges.

"I'll never turn that down. The mower is in the shed on the side of the house. Are you sure you have time for this?"

"Absolutely." He strolled toward the side of the house with the shed.

Anna slipped on her gloves. She hummed the melody to the old hymn "It Is Well With My Soul," as she tugged on a weed. It seemed the weeds of her life were almost taken care of, and in their place she sensed beauty like the newness of a spring flower.

Her troubles weren't gone yet, but the Lord was in control and she trusted all would be well.

Chapter Twenty-Two

Nancy pocketed her phone and looked around the park from her vantage point in the parking lot. Several preschool-age kids played on the jungle gym. A group of elementary-age kids played tag in the grass nearby, and a couple of dogs frolicked in the off-leash area—all in all a normal day at the park.

Lauren agreed to get her former boyfriend to meet her there, where Nancy would then pretend to be doing an interview for a human-interest story on the library's website. Police backup was in place and out of sight. If this went as planned, her friend would soon be able to breathe easy again.

Lauren pulled up in a car, parked, and got out. She waved to Nancy and rushed over to her. "I'm so nervous!"

"Relax. Your boyfriend's name is Isaac, right?"

"*Ex*-boyfriend, and yes—Isaac Bugler. Do you really think he's the person behind all the trouble Miss Plum has had?"

"I won't know for certain until I talk with him, but he's my best guess."

Lauren took a deep breath and let it out slowly. "Okay. I hope it's all right that I told my mom about this."

Nancy nodded. "Of course. Is she here somewhere?"

"No. Mom knows you from the library and trusts

you."

"Good." Nancy didn't know the girl's mom well but had spoken with the woman on several occasions through her years as the head librarian.

"Oh, there's Isaac." She waved to him.

Isaac looked like your everyday teenage boy with clean-cut brown hair and tall—tall enough to be on the basketball team. He didn't look at all like she'd imagined. He jogged over to them. "Hey." He shot Nancy a curious look.

"Hi." Lauren pointed toward a picnic table. "Should we sit over there?"

"Sounds good to me." Nancy headed in that direction, trusting the teens would follow. She heard them whispering behind her but couldn't decipher their words. Hopefully Lauren would stay cool and not ruin the plan. Nancy swung one leg over the bench then the other and sat.

The teens sat across from her. Lauren laced her fingers together and placed them on the picnic table in front of her.

Nancy pulled out a notepad and pen from her oversized purse and clicked the pen. "Thanks for meeting me. I'm really excited about this new feature on the library's website. Do you mind if I record this conversation so I don't miss anything?" She placed her smart phone on the table and waited.

"That's fine, I guess."

"Thanks."

Isaac nodded. "Why us? Lauren never said."

"Fair question. I met Lauren in Mr. Harms' English class when I was a guest speaker. We struck up a friendship of sorts, and she was the first person

I went to with my idea."

He shot Lauren a look and grinned. "Cool."

The girl smiled back. "I like your topic. Pressures teens face in the age of social media."

"Thanks." Nancy opened her notebook. "To begin with, how about telling me how the two of you met." She listened to a cute story of them bumping into one another in the hall at school. She nodded in the appropriate spots, biding her time until she could ask the real questions.

"After that, we kept seeing each other in the halls and then started eating lunch together," Lauren said.

"Yeah. Then I asked you out and the rest is history." Isaac frowned. "That is until you…"

"Until she what?" Nancy leaned slightly forward pen poised over the table.

He tilted his head. "Can I ask you a legit question?"

Nancy nodded. "I'll do my best to answer."

"I know your story is about social media and teens, and in a way, my question applies, but not directly."

"That's fine. Ask away, so long as you promise to return the favor."

"Sounds fair. I want to know why your generation thinks it's okay to dictate morality to my generation, when by your admission things are different than when you were a teenager."

Whoa. This kid didn't pull any punches. "I like your direct approach, but I need to understand where this question is coming from." She tried to keep her voice casual when she felt anything but. The anger flashing in his eyes and the set of his jaw alerted her to the importance of her answer.

"Off the record?" Isaac raised his chin.

"Okay." She glanced at Lauren who had turned a little pale.

"Lauren asked a teacher for advice about our relationship and was told to break up with me. I want to know why old people think they know what's best for my generation when they have no clue."

"Wow. That's a loaded question." She shot a glance to Lauren who now kept her head down. "Who is this teacher? You don't have to say, but I am curious."

A panicked look crossed his face before he masked it with indifference. "Miss Plum from the high school. I've seen you walking together. You friends with her?"

She nodded. "I am. Without knowing the specifics, I'd have to say that since my generation has lived longer than yours we feel like we speak from experience you don't yet have when we offer advice."

"But your experience is different from ours. You never dealt with the same pressures we do."

"I disagree." She kept her voice calm. "Yes, you face challenges I never had in high school. I believe the core of who we are and the issues we deal with are similar enough, that people my age and older have the knowledge and experience to hand out advice. And in all fairness to my friend, Lauren asked Miss Plum for advice, so it stands to reason she felt her suggestions were welcomed—not offensive."

"That's true, Isaac. I did ask Miss Plum for help, and she didn't *tell* me to break up with you."

His mouth opened. "But I thought you said—"

"I realized you thought that, and I let you believe it because it was easier. I should have cleared that up."

He ducked his head and groaned. "All this time I blamed Miss Plum." His face hardened. "It doesn't matter. It's still her fault. If she'd been more open-minded, then you would have never broken up with me."

"Would the two of you like some privacy?"

"It doesn't matter," Isaac said. "You can stay if Lauren is fine with it."

"I am." The girl reached out and took his hand. "Isaac?" She waited for him to look at her. "Did you try to get even with Miss Plum?"

His face crumpled. He looked to Nancy. "I want you to leave now."

She nodded but left her phone on the tabletop hoping he wouldn't remember that he'd agreed to have the conversation recorded. She stepped around a bush out of sight, but still close enough to hear the conversation.

"Please answer my question, Isaac," Lauren's voice shook. "Did you try to get even with Miss Plum?"

"What difference does it make? Anything I did, she had coming to her."

"No. She didn't do anything wrong. I made my own decision. What did you do?"

Nancy peered through a small hole in the bush toward the couple.

Lauren's gentle voice seemed to hold Isaac captive. "Please tell me Isaac." Lauren's gaze held his.

He sighed, never losing eye contact with the girl. "I hacked her computer at the school and messed with the writing contest."

Nancy didn't move and barely breathed, hoping he'd continue to forget about her phone recording their conversation. Lauren was amazing the way she had Isaac transfixed. Nancy hoped the wire she wore was recording his confession since he'd lowered his voice to a more intimate level.

"Is that all?"

He shook his head. "The more time that passed, the angrier I got. I did some mean stuff that I feel pretty bad about now."

"Are you the person who said she helped students cheat?"

"Yeah. I thought for sure they'd fire her. Then I'd be even. When they didn't, I got even angrier and did other stuff."

"I don't want you to be upset with her any more. Will you try to stop? For me?"

His face softened. "I suppose. Even though I feel bad about some of the stuff, it doesn't change how I feel. People need to mind their own business."

"I agree, but Miss Plum *was* minding her own business. I went to her because I trusted her. I knew she would be straight with me. I took what she said and made my own decision. I'm sorry you were hurt."

He stood. "I wish I'd never agreed to this. I can see by the look on your face that we will never be together now. Tell Nancy I don't want her to do the article. I thought I could make a difference. Be a voice for our generation, but it's hopeless now."

Lauren stood and faced him. "No it's not. Your voice can be heard. Let Nancy tell your story. Everyone will know the truth."

He stilled. "Why should I do that?"

"You said you wanted to make a difference. This can be your soapbox to let your voice be heard."

"But how can anything I've done help someone?" He stuffed his hands into his jeans pockets.

Nancy stepped out from behind the bush and walked toward the teens. "Mind if I join you again?"

Lauren shot her a nervous glance.

Isaac sighed. "Fine."

"Thanks. Are you ready to finish the interview?"

"I don't think anything I have to say will help your readers."

Nancy sat on the bench. "Let me tell your story, Isaac. I'm sure we can find a way to spin it so that your classmates will learn from your experience."

"I don't know. If word gets out about the things I've done, I could wind up in juvie. I won't talk about those things, but if you want to hear my thoughts on why people need to mind their own business and stuff then we can talk."

Nancy didn't want to let on that she'd been listening the entire time, and since he hadn't noticed her approach, he was clueless. "Okay. I guess that will have to do. Let's start with your age." Nancy asked.

"I'm seventeen."

"If at any time you change your mind we can stop. But I would like for you to tell me the whole story and let me write up a piece the people in this town won't soon forget."

He glanced toward Lauren as if asking what he should do. Little beads of sweat formed on his forehead. He took a breath and let it out in a puff. "I don't know. But either way I need to see the article and approve it before you post it. Deal?"

"I can accept that."

Nancy listened to an angry, hurting young man tell his tale of revenge, minus a few incriminating details. The hate that spewed from him was palpable. How could she spin this to be an uplifting article? The enormity of the task ahead almost overwhelmed her.

Isaac finally stopped talking and with a sigh, stood. "Now that you know about me I figure I only have one option."

"What's that?" Nancy held her breath.

"Turn myself in."

"I'll come with you." Lauren stood.

"No. I need to do this on my own. But thanks." He walked away.

Nancy expelled her breath in a whoosh. She hadn't seen that coming. She hoped the deputies would give him the opportunity to do what he said rather than confront him here in the park. At least he wouldn't know that Lauren had set him up. "You are a brave young woman, Lauren. I know it can't have been easy to stand up to Isaac."

"I've never been so scared in my life. When you told me your suspicions, I thought for sure you couldn't be right and that you'd walk away no closer to solving the mystery. I was wrong. Wow. It's so hard to imagine he did all of that. He's not a bad guy."

"I believe you. But anger and hate corrupt in inconceivable ways."

She nodded. "I should go home. I know my mom was anxious, even though she said she wasn't."

"Okay. Thanks again." She stood as Lauren

hustled toward the parking lot.

A moment later Carter strolled, out of uniform, toward Nancy. "Nice job. I gave Lyle a heads-up. One of the other deputies is following from a discrete distance to make sure he goes where he said."

"I kind of feel bad for the kid."

"That's because you're a softy." His eyes gleamed. "Are we still on for this weekend?"

"Of course." She tried to play it off as no big deal, but her breath caught for some reason. "What are we doing?"

"It's a surprise."

"You know how I feel about surprises."

"But you love a good mystery." He draped an arm across her shoulder. "Come on, I'll give you a lift home."

Chapter Twenty-Three

"I CAN'T BELIEVE ISAAC BUGLER IS responsible for everything." Anna sat in her living room with Nancy, Carter, and Luke. Luke was taking her out, and Nancy had shown up with Carter shortly before her date had arrived.

"I agree," Luke said. "He's an excellent student with great parents. If that conversation hadn't been recorded, I'm not sure I'd have believed it. Guess it shows you never truly know what a person is capable of."

"Yep." Carter said. "Nancy and I should be going. We didn't mean to interrupt your evening, but we knew Anna would want to know the mystery was solved."

They all stood and walked toward the entrance. Anna grabbed her purse and followed her friends out, locking up behind them. They parted ways in the driveway.

The enormity of everything they'd said struck her. "I'm in the mood to celebrate."

Luke opened the passenger side door. "Me too."

Anna sat in the seat and pulled out her phone. She shot off a text to Titus. "My tormentor turned himself in!" She pressed send as Luke eased in beside her.

"Everything okay?" He nodded toward her phone.

"Yes. I let Titus know about Isaac."

He frowned. "I thought there was nothing going on between the two of you."

"There's not. He's been a good friend through all of this, and I wanted him to know. I would have sent you a text too, if you hadn't been there when Carter and Nancy gave me the news."

He nodded and started his car. "Fair enough. I'm sorry for sounding jealous."

Anna grinned. "Were you jealous?"

"Uh..."

She laughed. "You don't have to answer that. Where are we going?"

"I thought we'd head to Salem for dinner and a movie."

"Sounds good to me." Her phone chimed an incoming message. She checked the screen. "It's from Titus. He said, what a relief. PTL." Praise the Lord indeed. She had a lot to be thankful for, and she couldn't wait to see what He had in store for her future—one she hoped included the man sitting beside her.

"Can I open my eyes yet?" Nancy held her hands to her face.

"Not yet," Carter said. "We're almost there." With his hands on each of her shoulders, he guided her forward over what felt like pavement.

"Where are we?"

"You'll see." He stopped. "Okay. Open your eyes."

"Is that what I think it is?" A blue 1969 Mustang

in need of a restoration sat in front of them. "Oh! My! Goodness! I think it's the same model I had."

"Yep. It needs some work, but the engine purrs."

"Whose is it?"

"Yours if you want it. If not, I know a certain young man chomping at the bit to take it off my hands."

She nearly exploded with excitement. "Yes! I'll take it. How much?"

"That's the best part. The guy selling it needed to make a quick buck. He offered me a great deal. Why not sit in it? See what you think."

A flash of light through the windshield caught her attention. "He left something hanging from the mirror." She two-stepped it toward the driver's side and slid in, leaving the door open. It didn't smell like her car, but a detail job could fix that. Her gaze landed on the object hanging from the rearview mirror on a red ribbon. "It's a ring!" She gasped. Turning her head, she found Carter on one knee beside the car's open door.

"It's a princess cut diamond ring to be exact. Will you hand it to me please?"

She reached for it then dropped it into his outstretched palm. Her pulse thundered through her ears. She'd figured he was going to propose soon, but wow!

Carter took her hand in his. "Nancy, I love you with all my heart. I can't imagine not having you in my life. Will you marry me?"

"Yes!"

He removed the ribbon from the ring and slid it onto her finger.

"It fits." Wonder filled her voice as she held out her hand, admiring the glistening ring. "How did you know my size?"

"Your mom helped." He stood and drew her from the car then pointed to her mom about ten feet away holding a video camera.

"She filmed this?"

"I know how you like to have everything on video."

She laughed and wrapped her arms around his neck. "I love you so much. Thank you for making this so incredible." She knew without a doubt he was the one—her dilemma was over.

"My pleasure." He captured her mouth with his, sealing their promise of a future together.

Author Notes

It's not often a writer has the privilege to write for a publisher that supports their writer's whims. Maybe 'whims' isn't the right word, but I so appreciate that my publisher was willing to take a risk on a new genre for me. I've always had a passion for books that included elements of mystery and suspense, and my publisher encouraged me in every book I've written for Mountain Brook Ink to follow that passion.

I never dreamed I would get to write a romantic mystery series. I had more fun than ever writing the second book in The Librarian Sleuth series. I hope you enjoyed reading it as much as I did writing it.

Will you take a moment to share your thoughts about this book in a review? I know that can be intimidating, but honestly, a one or two-line sentence about why you liked it is ideal. Since this is a mystery, giving anything away regarding the plot would spoil it for other readers. Thanks so much for your support in helping to spread the word about this book.

Blessings to you,
Kimberly Rose Johnson

If you want to post a review, any of the following places are appreciated: Amazon, Goodreads, ChristianBook.com, and Barnes and Noble.com

I'd love to connect with you! If you're online at all,

here are a few places you can find me and learn more about my books:

Kimberly's website: www.kimberlyrjohnson.com
Facebook: www.facebook.com/KimberlyRoseJohnson
Twitter: www.twitter.com/kimberlyrosejoh
Pinterest: www.pinterest.com/krose1990
Amazon: www.amazon.com/default/e/B00K10CR6E
BookBub:www.bookbub.com/authors/kimberly-rose-johnson

Don't miss the third book in this series, coming January 1, 2020. Paperback issue will release prior to Christmas, around December 15, 2019.

Books by Kimberly Rose Johnson

Brides of Seattle
The Reluctant Groom

Melodies of Love
A Love Song for Kayla
An Encore for Estelle
A Waltz for Amber

Sunriver Dreams
A Love to Treasure
A Christmas Homecoming
Designing Love

Wildflower B&B Romance Series
Island Refuge
Island Dreams
Island Christmas
Island Hope

Contemporary Inspirational Romance Collection
In Love and War

Contemporary Novella
Brewed with Love

www.ingramcontent.com/pod-product-compliance
Lightning Source LLC
Chambersburg PA
CBHW070635170726
48291CB00003B/1031